D1383505

Blue Coyote

LIZA KETCHUM

Blue Coyote

SIMON & SCHUSTER BOOKS FOR YOUNG READERS

YA
KET

ACKNOWLEDGMENTS:

For their wise and generous counsel, and assistance with many aspects of this book, I am grateful to: Eileen Christelow, Michael Conathan, Miriam Dror, David Gale, Nancy Garden, Gavin Harrison, Karen Hesse, Carey Johnson, Dylan Leiner, Katherine Leiner, Bob MacLean, Ashley Mason, and John Straus. Thanks to the women at Duxbury House, who provided an inspiring space to write, and to David Fitzgerald and his customers at Fitzy's Tattoo Shop, in Hinsdale, New Hampshire, who were patient while I observed, asked questions, and absorbed information about the ancient art of tattooing. Finally, I am particularly grateful to Brian Dougherty and Michael Fernandes for their sensitive and careful responses to my questions, as well as to the manuscript at various stages.

SIMON & SCHUSTER BOOKS FOR YOUNG READERS
An imprint of Simon & Schuster Children's Publishing Division
1230 Avenue of the Americas, New York, New York 10020
Copyright © 1997 by Liza Ketchum

Book design by Anahid Hamparian
The text for this book is set in 12-point Elegant Garamond
Printed and bound in the United States of America

First Edition
10 9 8 7 6 5 4 3 2 1
Library of Congress Cataloging-in-Publication Data
Ketchum, Liza.
p.   cm.
Summary: While searching for his lost friend, Alex not only learns the reasons behind Tito's disappearance but also comes to accept some hidden truths about himself.
ISBN 0-689-80790-2
[1. Homosexuality—Fiction. 2. Identity—Fiction. 3. Self-acceptance—Fiction.] I. Title.
PZ7.K488B1 1997
[Fic]—dc20   96-19913

For Bob, Eileen, and Karen:
dear friends and partners on the journey
—L. K.

PART ONE

SPRING

GRISWOLD, VERMONT

I dream I'm with Tito again. We walk barefoot through thick fog, hurrying across the cold pavement in the parking lot. Tiny waves thump against the packed sand. The beach is empty, except for the old guy with the grizzled beard who sweeps the beach with his metal detector, searching for coins.

We cross the bike path. A lone biker hums past, head tucked, as he pedals south.

Tito throws a towel across a wet bench. We sit to pull on our Rollerblades, cinch them tight. I lean back while Tito skates to the concrete plaza, sets his tape deck on an overturned garbage can. He wheels slowly, casually, carving wide circles on the pavement like a figure skater on clean ice. My eyes follow his moves; he's fluid, graceful for such a stocky guy. He catches me watching, grins and cups a hand to his ear. I shove Red Hot Chili Peppers into the box, jack up the volume, then warm up, my skates carving a slow square frame around Tito's fast strides. Our wheels chatter on the concrete. Tito whistles. His black eyes meet mine. I catch the dare in his quick smile and nod. I'm ready.

We slide into our routine: a dance on wheels. We weave in and out, skim close but don't touch. Figure eights and tucks. Arms pump, then fling wide, arching the chest. I crouch low, whirl on one foot, rise into a double spin. Tito imitates me, then surges backward through an obstacle course of soda bottles, cardboard boxes, broken beach chairs. I follow.

Suddenly, he catches me by the waist, spins me around, lets me fly. I almost lose it, but catch myself and turn. We nearly collide. Tito grabs my elbows as our legs brace wide, feet turned out to trace the rim of a lazy circle. His hands slide down my arms, fingers make tight bracelets around my wrists while his eyes search mine. He's trying to tell me something. His mouth opens, but nothing comes out. He gives me a desperate look, then twists away and takes off up the bike path, heading north. Stocky arms swing side to side like a speed skater, chin tucked, bare legs shove out from the center. I push off, chasing him.

The fog lifts. The emerald green Santa Monica Mountains tumble into the Pacific. Tito's a small dynamo, whirling up a concrete ribbon in the sand.

His name catches in my throat. I scream an empty sound.

He skates faster, flashing legs driving. We pass deserted parking lots, the playground, Muscle Beach. I'm gasping for breath. I know what's ahead.

Waves smash and curl around the dark pylons of the pier. My voice finally bursts from my chest like a raspy hinge. "Tito, wait!"

He flicks me a wave but doesn't turn. I lunge forward, too late. The wet cave under the pier swallows him up.

I hesitate, then skate in after him, slowing to adjust to the dim light. The path snakes through the pylons, greased and gleaming with slime. Winos lurk in the shadows, bottles hidden in paper sacks. A rough voice calls out: Hey kid, spare some change? A truck rumbles overhead, rattling the boards like a stick running along an iron fence. A biker hurtles toward me, swerves and swears. I lose my balance, stumble into the sand. Hot breath at my neck, stubby fingers grope for my pocket.

I slap the hand away, scramble for the pavement and lurch to my feet, striding toward the golden square of sunlight. I burst into the open, lungs burning, and coast to a stop. The bike path stretches to the north, clean, empty, and shining. Tito is gone.

One

Alex Beekman woke with his heart pounding, his sheets clammy with sweat. He lay still, yearning for the sound of waves hissing on sand, but an annoying chorus of tree frogs told him he was still stuck in the nowhere town of Griswold, Vermont, three thousand miles from the Pacific Ocean.

"Damn." Alex clenched his fists and rolled over, burying his face in the pillow. Was someone sending this dream to torture him? He'd had it over and over in the last two months, ever since Tito had disappeared.

Alex glanced at the luminous numbers on his watch: one in the morning. He threw off the covers and sat up against the wall. He'd never get back to sleep now. He was all wound up, and his bones ached from growing pains. The last time Dad measured him on the door frame beside the stairs, he was six foot three, but that was a few months ago. Now his pants were too short again, and his toes hurt from being wedged against the ends of his running shoes.

But it wasn't the pain in his joints that kept him awake. It was the dull ache in his chest, the anxious thoughts zipping through his skull, ramming into each other like bumper cars on the Santa Monica pier. Why had Tito Perone, his best friend in the world, dropped out of his life?

Until March, he and Tito talked once or twice a week—giving their parents money when they complained about the bills—keeping their friendship alive. They both hated the phone, but they kept it up anyway. During their last call, Tito's list of exploits was longer than usual, and he spoke in a low voice so his parents wouldn't hear. "I've been hang gliding," he'd said. "Next time you come out, you'll have to try it. It's like surfing the air. I got my ear pierced at a tattoo shop—my mom really hit the ceiling on that one." Tito's voice fell to a whisper. "Beekman, you won't believe this—two more weeks of work and I'll have enough money for a motorcycle. Then I'll really be able to—" He'd stopped in mid-sentence, cleared his throat, and suddenly changed the subject. Alex figured someone had come into the room. He couldn't remember anything else about the conversation—but when he'd called a few days later, Tito was gone.

Or so it seemed. Alex had dialed the Perones' number over and over. No one was ever home, and Alex left a string of messages, some curt, some lengthy, some funny—but Tito never called back.

It had been two months now. What had he done wrong? Alex stared at the sloping ceiling over his bed. He was tortured by Tito's unfinished sentence. What did he plan to do, once he'd bought the cycle? Run away? But Tito wouldn't do that without telling Alex—would he? After all, they still had their secret dream: to take a year off after high school, work until they'd earned enough money, fly to Hawaii, surf the Pipeline.

But maybe Tito's plans had changed. Maybe he had new friends—but so what? Alex had been hanging out at Molly O'Connor's house almost every day since he'd moved to Griswold—but that didn't change the way he felt about Tito.

Sometime in April, Alex had written him a short letter, asking for an explanation. Nothing came back. He'd called the phone company, to make sure the number still belonged to the Perones, which it did. After that, he gave up.

Alex pulled his long T-shirt down over his boxers, opened his door softly, and stood on the landing, listening. No telling who was up. His family was famous for prowling around at night except for Dale, his mother, who always went to sleep early. Soft music played in his twin sister Rita's room, but she might have dozed off with the radio on.

He didn't want Rita to know what he was doing. Since they were tiny, she'd been able to slip into his thoughts. But there were a few things even Rita hadn't picked up on, and this mess with Tito was one of them. It had to stay private.

Alex edged downstairs, hugging the wall to avoid creaks, and went into the kitchen. The door to the basement stood open, and the lights were on. His father's off-key humming followed the uneven clicking of the computer keys. Chris Beekman had the weird habit of listening to saccharine movie scores while he wrote scripts. He claimed part of his brain was always ready to goof off, but if he fed it junk through his headphones, it freed up the creative part of his mind.

And then his father complained because his scripts ended up on TV, rather than in film. No wonder, Alex thought. If *he* listened to that crap while he was drawing, something boring would ooze onto his sketch pad, for sure.

Alex shrugged. At least his father wouldn't hear him talking. He carried the portable phone into the tiny den and punched in the number. The phone rang for a long time, and he was about to hang up when Tito's mother finally answered, sounding sleepy. A human voice, for once! Alex nearly dropped the phone.

"Hello, Alex," Mrs. Perone said when he told her who he was. Her voice was cool and polite.

"Is Tito there?" he asked.

She was quiet so long, the hair on the back of his neck began to prickle. "No," she said at last, "he isn't."

Alex cleared his throat. "Will he be home later?"

Again, she didn't answer. *What's wrong!* Alex wanted to scream, but he waited, his knees bouncing, picking at the worn chair fabric with his free hand. Finally, Mrs. Perone said, with a kind of fierce calm, "Tito doesn't live here anymore."

She made it sound as if Tito were just some guy who rented a room in their house. Alex paced the tiny room, the cordless phone pressed tight to his ear. "You mean—he moved out?"

"We asked him to leave. Tito did something unforgivable. Until he comes around, he's no longer a member of the family."

Alex blinked hard to keep back tears. "Could you—do you have his phone number?"

"No." Mrs. Perone sounded annoyed now. "He's in L.A. somewhere. You could try information."

Jesus. Questions piled up in Alex's mind, skidding out of control like cars on a slick freeway. Did Tito leave the Catholic Church for good? End up in the ER one too many times? Wreck his dad's Chevy? Maybe. But his family wouldn't kick him out for that. They always complained their car was a heap. Besides, boys were a big deal for the Perones, and Tito was their only son. Out of their *lives?* Forget it. Unless—

But no. Alex wouldn't think about that last possibility. "I—I don't understand," he stammered at last.

"Are you sure?" Mrs. Perone's icy voice was scary. "I thought you, of all people—" she paused. "Never mind. I'm sorry I can't help you, Alex. And now, if you'll excuse me, I'd like to go back to sleep."

Alex apologized and turned off the phone. He sat at the table a long time, staring at the poster he'd tacked on the wall when they first arrived in Vermont. It showed a surfer on a six-foot triple scag, disappearing into the tube on Oahu's famous Pipeline. The wave was at least a double, maybe a triple overhead. Even though Alex didn't have the strength or the skills to surf those twenty-foot monsters, he would have tried—if Tito dared him to. Maybe Perone had gone to Hawaii without him. Alex couldn't stand that idea. And anyway he didn't see how Tito could afford it.

Alex tried information for all three Los Angeles area codes, but no one had a listing for Tito Perone.

He tossed the phone onto the sagging couch. The more he tried to imagine what Tito could have done to make his parents so angry, the more agitated he felt. He scooped up Bunter, their marmalade cat, and held him tight, but the cat sank his claws into his chest. "Ouch!" Alex pushed him away. He went to the fridge, poured himself a glass of milk, and drank it standing up, staring at the ugly beige door. His family didn't stay anywhere long enough to collect stuff on the fridge. Only his and Rita's school photos stared back at him, their blue eyes matching the navy backdrop the photographer had used. Rita had given the photographer her most magnetic smile, while Alex looked worried, tense. As usual. The thought of school made his chest feel tighter than ever.

"Hey, Alex, what's up?"

Alex jumped, slopping milk on the floor. He turned around. Rita stood in the doorway, her hair loose down her back, wearing one of his old T-shirts. "Damn it, Rita—you scared me."

"Sorry. I heard you talking. Were you on the phone?"

Alex nodded. "Let's go upstairs," he whispered.

They went to his room, closed the door, and huddled on the bed. Alex pulled his blankets around his shoulders.

"Cold?" Rita asked, nestling close to him.

"A little," Alex said, but it wasn't the temperature. He leaned against the wall. No use keeping it a secret now. "I called the Perones. They've kicked Tito out of the house."

Rita pulled back, her eyes darkening. "You're kidding. Why?"

"Mrs. Perone wouldn't tell me. Said he'd done something 'unforgivable'—whatever that means. Claims she doesn't even know where he *lives*, for Christ's sake." Alex thought of Mrs. Perone's accusing tone. "She was weird. She made it sound as though I should know what's going on."

"What could he have done? He was never into drugs. Maybe—" Rita ducked her head. Her long hair made a veil across her face. "Maybe he got someone pregnant." Her voice trembled.

"I doubt it." Alex studied his sister. Why was she so freaked? He couldn't read her. His own twin antennae must be messed up. "Tito's mom said he wasn't a member of their family. If he knocked someone up—they'd be pissed, but not like this."

Rita tossed her hair back and looked him in the eye. "Don't talk about it like that."

"Sorry." Alex pulled her close. He remembered Tito telling him about hang gliding, about piercing his ear—who knows what else he had tried? "He must have pulled too many wild stunts." But Alex knew that couldn't be it. A cold, icy trickle settled into his gut. He tried to ignore it.

"What should we do?" Rita whispered.

"I don't know. We can't let him disappear."

Rita was quiet for a long time. Finally she said, "Maybe that's how he wants it."

Alex sat up straight. "What do you mean?"

She picked at the blanket. "I kind of wondered—why we hadn't heard from him in so long." Her cheeks were flushed. "I wrote him some letters—but he never answered."

Alex pulled back so he could see his sister's face. "I never knew that." He hadn't thought of Rita and Tito being close— but why not? After all, Perone practically lived at the Beekmans' for five years, following them from one house to another all over L.A.

"I thought he'd forgotten about us," Rita said. "Now I wonder if he even got my letters." She gave Alex a shy smile. "I had a crush on Tito for a long time."

Alex grinned. Man, he really *had* lost the knack of twin ESP. "Did Tito know?"

"I don't think so. He was clueless." She leaned her head against his shoulder. They were quiet for a long time. Alex shut his eyes, remembering the day he'd met Tito. It was February, five years ago. As usual, their family had moved right in the middle of the year. Their new school was only four blocks from the beach, and the kids ate lunch on the asphalt playground outside. Alex and Rita sat alone at a long table. They didn't know a soul.

Rita nudged him, breaking into his thoughts. "Remember that day in sixth grade, when Tito showed you how to surf on our lunch table?"

Alex groaned. "Unbelievable. How did you know what I was thinking?" He kept his eyes closed. "What do you see, when you think about that day?"

"Sun on the whitecaps—and the bougainvillea vine, covered with pink flowers—I thought they were made of paper."

Alex nodded. What he remembered most vividly was this stocky kid with jet-black hair slicked back from his forehead who'd flung open the school door, caught Alex's eye, and pushed toward them through the lines of tables, carrying his tray high over his head. He'd plunked himself down next to Alex as if the twins had saved him a seat.

He'd asked if Alex knew how to surf, and when Alex said he'd like to learn, Tito had pushed his food away and jumped onto his lunch tray as if it were a surfboard. He'd settled into a surfer's stance, right there on the table. Even then, his legs were as muscular as a man's. His hips swiveled, and his arms went out for balance. "Up and over the lip!" he'd cried. "Into an aerial." The tray slid down the table and shot off the end. Alex had jumped up, expecting Tito to fall on his back, but he landed on both feet like a cat and flashed Alex a smile. He stuck out his hand to introduce himself, and Alex noticed his eyes were so dark, the irises melted into the pupils. "Meet me after school," Tito had said. "We'll see about getting you a stick."

"A stick?" Alex had asked stupidly.

"A board." Tito pointed to the surfboard flying across his purple T-shirt. "So you can surf."

Tito left without touching his lunch. Alex had watched him walk away, unable to explain the disturbing feelings inside. Still, as Tito disappeared around the corner of the building, Alex decided that Los Angeles was wonderful. And if his father made them move again, he'd never forgive him.

Now, here they were on the other side of the country. "If Dad hadn't brought us to Vermont, we wouldn't have lost him," Alex said.

Rita didn't answer. Alex looked down at his sister's head, her hair shining in the lamplight, and remembered something else about that first meeting. Even when Rita was still just a skinny kid, most boys were drawn to her like a magnet. But Tito acted, that first time, as if she didn't exist.

"Mrs. Perone said Tito was in L.A.," Alex said quietly.

Rita's voice was muffled. "Big help," she said. "Surrounded by millions of other people." She sat up and looked at him. "You know him better than anyone. You can't guess what he did wrong?"

"No way." Alex turned away, remembering his dream. Tito seemed desperate to tell him something. What could it be? He shoved the last, scary possibility behind the cold, steel door where he hid his darkest thoughts, and wrapped his arms around his knees. "Forget sleeping tonight."

"Lie down. I'll be right back." Rita slipped out of the room.

Alex slid between the sheets and lay on his back, waiting. The lamp beside his bed threw shadows on his latest art project, pinned up on the wall. It was a poster-sized colored-pencil drawing of a hawk circling high over its prey: a tiny field mouse, scurrying toward a live oak through grass as long and silky as his sister's hair. The art teacher had liked it, but she kept urging Alex to draw what he observed. She didn't understand that Alex drew what he saw in his mind—and it was always California.

Rita came back with her flute and sat near his feet. She played a soft, jazzy riff, something she'd adapted from a Jethro Tull song. The notes washed over him in the dark like ocean swells, rising and falling with his breath. He twisted the ring Tito had given him when he left L.A. last fall, willing it to send him a message.

There must be some way to find Perone. Unless Rita was right—and he didn't want to be found. When they were younger, Tito loved to lead Alex on a wild-goose chase through dusty canyons on their dirt bikes. He would disappear into the chaparral where Alex didn't dare go because he was afraid of rattlesnakes. If Tito wanted to disappear, he would. And there was no way in hell Alex could ever find him.

TWO

Spring fever raged in room twenty-nine the next afternoon. Alex was late for study hall, and he heard the buzz of talk and laughter long before he reached the door. He crumpled his excuse in his palm when he saw Ms. Schuman's chair was empty. Students lounged on each other's desks, leaned out the open windows to smoke, tossed a soft football from one end of the room to the other. In the far corner, Randy Tovitch shook a bottle of Coke until it fizzed, held it out from his body, and twisted the cap. Warm liquid spewed onto the pink blouse of the girl sitting in front of him. She shrieked and ran for the door, knocking into Alex as if he were invisible.

If only he *could* disappear, Alex thought. Tovitch made him sick. What was he doing in study hall? Usually Randy spent his free periods in the caf, near the soda machine, or outside the back door, sneaking a smoke. Alex was tempted to leave before Tovitch noticed him, but he'd never been caught for skipping class, and detention was even worse than this scene. Alex tried to slip unnoticed into an empty seat near the door, but Tovitch spotted him.

"Hey, Beekman! Be a good *girl* and watch for Schuman, will you?"

A couple of kids snickered. Alex ignored them. His eyes burned from being up half the night. He wanted to put his head down and sleep, but Randy sent Dex, his skinhead side-kick, out into the hall to play sentry, then sauntered over, pulling long swigs from his soda as if it were a beer. Alex took

out his sketch pad and a pen and began drawing aimless
circles.

"Been pumping iron? Making yourself more beautiful for
the *guys?*" Randy faked a lisp and let his hand dangle limp at
his side. Alex bent over his pad, the circular sketches becom-
ing a turtle. Not the placid sea turtle that decorated his surfboard, but a snapping turtle who could take off Randy's arm
with one bite. Alex drew the turtle's long, leathery neck, its
sharp, angular jaw jutting open. Randy leaned over Alex's
desk and slopped Coke onto his drawing. "Oh, *so* sorry!" he
said, his tone fake and sweet. "Did I wreck your pretty
picture?"

Alex wanted to tell Randy just what he could do with himself, and where, but he refused to sink to Tovitch's level. "Bug
off," he said.

Randy laughed and kept moving, cruising toward a small
group of girls at the back of the room. No matter what Alex
did, Tovitch found a way to make his life miserable. When
Alex started using the weight room, sometime in January, he'd
thought he'd finally discovered a place to be alone. He liked
the rhythm of the weight machines, the challenge of setting
small goals for himself, the feel of his muscles gaining strength
and power, particularly in his upper body.

He worked out in the afternoons, when Tovitch was away
at ski meets. But then Randy flunked math and was kicked off
the Alpine team. Before long, he was hanging out in the
weight room, too, flaunting his prowess, especially if there
were other guys watching. Lately, Alex felt he had no place to
hide except the art room—and it was rarely empty.

"Hold it!" Dex poked his shaved head around the door
frame, then raised his hand. The room quieted, students
poised to make a dive for their desks. "New kid," he said. "A
real shrimp—coming our way."

A new guy, in the middle of *May?* Rough. Even the

Beekmans had never moved at such a bad time. Alex was curious, and when the kid stood in the doorway, looking confused, Alex's mouth went dry. Was he the image of Tito, or what? Same snapping eyes, dark hair slicked back, olive skin—same swarthy, muscular body and tight jeans—

Alex twisted the wide silver band on his finger and stared openly. The kid was short, but otherwise, the resemblance was uncanny.

Then the guy smiled, a cocky grin showing a wide mouth, and Alex realized he didn't look like Tito at all. He turned away, embarrassed, but it was too late: The kid had caught him staring. He came over and plunked his computerized schedule on Alex's desk. "Is this room thirty-six?" he asked. "Calculus?"

Alex shook his head and studied the printout. Klema, David, it read. Class: Junior. Calculus, already? So the kid was smart. Most juniors—Alex included—were taking trig. "It's down the hall, through the connector." A paper airplane sailed between them, and the room erupted in hoots. Alex pushed back his chair and grabbed his books. "This is the *fourth*-grade room today. Come on, I'll show you where to go."

To his horror, Tovitch let loose with a wolf whistle as they left. "Love at first sight," Randy cried.

Alex shut the door hard and turned up the collar on his rugby shirt, hoping the guy couldn't see the blush spreading up his neck.

"What was *that* about?" the new kid asked.

"Just Tovitch, the school's number one asshole," Alex said, trying to sound casual. He glanced down at the kid. He had unusual hazel eyes, with golden flecks that seemed splashed on, and his smile was easy, friendly. What the hell, Alex thought. Might as well fill him in. "Tovitch is still pissed at me from last fall. Thinks I stole his spot on the soccer team."

"Did you?" The kid's grin widened.

"Not really. He kept his position. But he got bent out of shape—"

"I take it you're good."

Alex shrugged, too modest to tell this stranger the truth: He'd ended the year as top scorer, taking the team to the state finals. Tovitch had never forgiven him for stealing his glory. "Three of us forwards played well," he said. "Me, Todd O'Connor, and Tovitch, who's a good athlete, even if he is an asshole. And our sweeper, Craig, is excellent—you'll meet him, too. Tovitch will be gone next season, if he graduates—a big IF. Rumor has it some teachers will pass him just so they never see him again." Alex stopped, embarrassed by how much he was talking. Sure, he was starved for friendship—but did he have to make it so obvious? Then the guy surprised him by sticking out his hand. "I'm David Klema, officially. But I go by Klema."

"I'm Alex. Alex Beekman." They shook, and Alex smiled. It was a relief to talk to someone who wasn't about to stab him in the back. They walked slowly down the hall. "We're fairly new in town, too," Alex told him. "Came last fall. Where you from?"

"New York," the kid said. "Brooklyn. And you?"

"L.A., and a few other places. We've moved a lot."

"So what's it like here?" Klema asked. "What do people do for fun?"

Alex stopped in the middle of the hall. "You really want to know?"

"I guess." Klema laughed nervously.

"It's kind of grim," Alex said. "In Griswold, a big thrill is a party where the parents are gone for the weekend and someone buys a keg with a fake ID. Most guys spend Saturdays under the hood of a pickup, or they work at Crystal Hill—that's the local ski area—putting flatlanders on the lift."

Klema flashed him a crooked smile. "Flatlanders. That's

me, I guess. It's weird—I've been snowboarding at Crystal Hill. We rented a condo near the mountain once, in a flush year. I never thought I'd be here as a local."

Alex didn't want to spoil Klema's day by telling him he'd be an outsider forever if he wasn't born here. Instead, he said, "People think Griswold is the whole world. When my family goes to Boston or New York for an orgy of movies, the neighbors think we're nuts." Alex stopped. He was sounding like a snob—but he couldn't help it. He'd never fit in here.

Alex showed Klema the way through the connector, a long enclosed bridge linking the old brick building to the newer, cinder block addition. "How come you moved?" Alex said. "Your parents change jobs?"

Klema shifted his book to the other hip. "Sort of." He hesitated. "It's just me and my mom."

"Sorry," Alex said. "I didn't mean to be nosy. My parents move all the time, so I'm curious."

"No problem." Klema's smile came easily and often. "How many moves?"

"Would you believe fifteen?"

Klema looked up at him, whistling softly. "Man, that's bad. Fifteen schools?"

"No. Sometimes just a new house or apartment. We actually lived in Los Angeles almost five years, but in seven different places. My dad always thinks things will be better somewhere else." He glanced at Klema. "Of course, I wouldn't mind being back in L.A. myself right now."

"You a surfer?" Klema asked.

"Yeah." Alex let it go at that. No need to explain Tito's disappearance to a total stranger.

"My mom sure picked a swell time to move," Klema said. "End of junior year." He sighed. "Guess I can stand anything for a year. But when I graduate—I'm out of here. Back to the city."

"Yeah, me, too," Alex said, but he suddenly felt lost. Going back to L.A. had always meant picking up Tito, heading out to Hawaii. Maybe that was just a fantasy—but it was a nice one. Now Perone had messed up their dream and tossed it aside, leaving Alex with a rank, bitter taste in his mouth.

He stopped outside the calculus room. "This is it," he told Klema. "Sorry if I made you late. Ms. Foster is tough, but she's fair—I have her for trig. Good luck."

"Thanks. Hey, see you around?"

"Sure." Alex ducked his chin to hide his pleasure. When he looked up, Klema had straightened his back, as if to make himself look taller, and was striding into the classroom. Alex was impressed. Whenever he was in a tense situation, he always wished he could shrink so no one would notice him. Klema was introducing himself to Ms. Foster as though it were normal to come cruising into a new school four weeks before the end of the year.

Alex shifted his pack to his other shoulder and went back through the connector, checking his watch. Study hall was half over, and the thought of dealing with Tovitch made his stomach muscles clench up. The hell with class, Alex thought. He'd use the bench press for a while. If he was caught, he'd deal.

He took the inner staircase down two flights, avoiding the corridor that passed the main office, and walked along the narrow hall to the gym, hoping no sharp-eared teacher would hear the lonely squeak of his shoes on linoleum. He made it to his gym locker without anyone noticing and was about to strip to shorts and a T-shirt when he heard a familiar laugh at the end of the row of lockers. He whirled around and found himself face-to-face with Tovitch and his two cohorts: Benji, a big kid with hands like bear paws, and that idiot, Dex, who did everything Tovitch told him to.

"Thought you'd be here," Randy said. "Had to cool down, right?"

Alex slammed his locker door and pinched the lock to close it. So much for the weight room. "Why don't you just say what you mean and get it over with."

Randy leered, his capped tooth gleaming. "I saw the way you looked at that guy—as if he were the new *girl* in town. Gave you a hard-on, didn't he?"

"Jesus." Alex grabbed his pack and hopped over the wooden bench, headed for the door, but Tovitch caught his arm, pulling him toward the shower room.

"Come on guys," Tovitch said. "Let's ice him down."

"Hey!" Alex tried to twist away, but Dexter was on his other arm, his foul breath close to his nose, and Benji grabbed his belt from behind, shoving him forward. Alex managed a kick to Dex's knee, pushing him off, but he couldn't shake Randy or Benji. His shirt ripped under the arms.

"Turn on the showers!" Randy shouted as they yanked Alex across the slippery tiles. Dexter ran ahead, twisting the handles on the first three showers, aiming the heads at the center of the room. Randy gave him a final shove and Alex fell into the middle, spluttering and pushing his pack away to keep it out of the water, scrambling for a safe hold as if he were on ice.

"Hold him under!" Randy yelled. "Get him clean! We don't want to catch what he's got!"

Suddenly, a deep voice behind them called out, "What the *hell* is going on here?"

Tovitch, Dexter, and Benji froze, then scattered. Alex lunged to his feet and scrambled away from the gushing faucets, gasping for breath. Mr. Grayson, the head of the athletic department, glared at him. "What's the story, Beekman?" he demanded.

"Ask them," Alex sputtered, jerking his thumb toward Tovitch. But the shower room was empty, and the door at the end of the locker room flapped open. Alex swore.

"Hold it just a minute," Grayson said, but Alex scooped up his pack and darted past him, running along the tops of the long benches to the door that led to the gym. He raced across the empty basketball court, his shoes leaving wet tracks on the shiny floorboards, and ducked behind the bleachers, huddling in the shadows until his breath no longer came in long, shuddering sobs. When the first bell shrilled, he waited for the stampede in the halls, then slipped out the back door, running even faster this time.

"Alex!" Rita's voice rang out, but he didn't stop. He had to get away before Randy showed up. It would only take Tovitch a few seconds to fill his truck with deadbeats who'd love to hunt him down. Alex darted between parked cars, raced to unlock his bike, and peddled up Main Street as if the cops were after him.

three

Alex skidded in the mud at the top of the drive-way and swerved onto the grass to avoid his mother's station wagon. What was she doing home so early? Usually Dale didn't get back from the bank until five-thirty. Dad's Honda was here as usual; he'd been downstairs in his office a lot lately, finishing the pilot for a new TV show.

Alex dropped his bike in the grass, started up the long flight of stairs to the porch, and then stopped, his hand gripping the wobbly railing. His parents were arguing inside the A-frame. He turned around slowly and sat near the bottom of the stairs, resting his head on his bent knees. He'd been hoping for an empty house so he could cool down alone.

He took a couple of long, deep breaths. Thank God it was Friday. How could he show his face in school Monday? Not to mention the day after . . . and how many days left? He ticked off the weeks in his head. With Memorial Day, honor assemblies, and exams—less than four weeks. Four weeks of hell. And then what? A long, empty summer, with no job— he'd been looking, but nothing had come up yet—and no one to hang out with but Molly, who was great, but still. . . .

The new kid, Klema, seemed like a good guy, someone who could even be a friend. But Alex knew it couldn't last. He picked at a long splinter on the porch step. He'd give Tovitch a few days or a week, max. Randy would tell Klema some sick story about Alex, and the friendship would be over before it began. No doubt about it.

So he'd be stuck alone in Griswold for the summer, knowing his best friend had disappeared on the other side of the country. There must be someone he could call to get information about Tito—maybe his sisters? But Raquel Perone had gone off to college somewhere, and Sofia was married, living in the Northwest.

His legs twitched. Alex jumped up, found his soccer ball under the porch, and juggled the ball from knee to knee. The steady slap of leather on skin usually soothed him, but today it didn't work. He kept losing the rhythm. Finally he kicked the ball angrily into the thick stand of pines near the porch and watched it roll away into the shadows.

He was about to go in after it when the shadows under the branches seemed to darken, reminding him of a recurring nightmare that had followed him here from L.A. In the dream, he was standing at the edge of the La Brea Tar Pits, which once swallowed dinosaurs and saber-toothed tigers, encasing them in oil that preserved their skeletons, intact, for centuries. He always slipped at the edge, sliding into the viscous oil. . . .

Alex rubbed his eyes. Why the hell was he seeing this in broad daylight? Was he going nuts?

The ping of stones against wire brought him back to reality. Rita wheeled into the driveway and skidded in the mud as he had, but she recovered gracefully. She hopped off her bike and leaned it up against the station wagon. Her face was beet red, and her hair had come loose from its long braid. As she came closer, he saw she was upset as well as hot.

"Hard ride?" he called.

She stomped past and started for the stairs, but Alex spread his arms, blocking her way. "Hold on—what's the matter?"

Her eyes blazed. "You *knew* I was following you. Why didn't you wait?"

Alex perched on the stairs so his eyes were level with hers.

"Tovitch and his buddies jumped me in the locker room. They gave me a cold shower. I was afraid they'd chase after me."

"Damn." Rita's expression softened. "So that's why Randy was bugging me after school, asking where you'd gone."

"What did you say?"

She wiped her forehead with the tail of her T-shirt. "I lied. Told him you had a dentist appointment. Then he tried to sweet-talk me into his truck." Her long fingers twitched her hair from side to side, braiding it again. "What's Randy's problem, anyway?"

"Who knows. Guess he has to remind everyone he's an asshole, in case we've forgotten."

Rita twisted a rubber band around the end of her braid. "Is it the same old stuff?"

Alex nodded. "Once someone decides to call you a fag, you can't escape. It's like wearing the scarlet letter, except mine is a giant *F*." He avoided Rita's eyes. She sat on the step below him. The house was quiet; wind sighed in the pines.

"If anyone is gay, it's Randy Tovitch," Rita said suddenly.

"Come on." Alex stared at her. "Get serious."

"I am! Molly and I talked about it. He's so uptight about how macho he is. And he never has a date—"

Alex stiffened. "Hey, neither do I. Does that mean I'm gay, too?"

"Of course not," Rita said quickly.

"Besides, what girl in her right mind would go out with Randy Tovitch? I don't see *you* running after him."

She smiled. "Obviously I can't stand the guy. Especially after the way he's treated you. But there are some girls who like him, believe it or not. He's not that bad looking."

Alex shook his head in disbelief. Tovitch was one ugly dude, in his opinion. "I didn't know bushy eyebrows and chipped teeth turned you on."

Rita ignored him. "I still think it's weird. Randy only asks me out when there are other guys around. He knows I'll never accept. It's like he does it to prove he likes girls."

Alex nudged her back with his knees. "Rita, that's bull. He'd take you out in a second if you'd go, just like any other guy in this town." He leaned against the wall of the house. "You know, until last night, I couldn't figure out why you always turned them down. I was pretty clueless about you and Tito. Sorry."

She turned her face up to him, her eyes soft with tears. "Guess that's hopeless now, huh?"

Alex shrugged. "Who knows." He reached down to massage her shoulders, when their parents' voices suddenly rose from inside the house. They froze.

"You promised," their mother cried, her voice hard and shrill. "No . . . more . . . moves . . . For God's sake, Chris, we've only been here nine months. I'm just starting to meet people—"

Their father muttered something about a "big break this time." Rita moved up next to Alex and wedged herself in beside him. "Not again," she moaned.

Alex wrapped his arm around his sister and held tight. A heavy stone settled against his rib cage as they listened. The fight was familiar. Like a theme song from a movie, it repeated itself over and over every few years, sometimes in a minor key, sometimes a major, but always with the same resolution: a new town, a new neighborhood, a new house or school, someplace where their father would be able to write "legitimate theater," or "serious dramatic films," as he put it, instead of scripts for lousy TV shows. Their mother always complained, then pulled herself together, talked to real estate agents, found a house or an apartment and a steady job that paid the bills, usually in a bank or as a CPA. But Dad had promised that this move was different, the end of the line.

Alex sat up. What if—

But no. He didn't dare think that way. He'd only jinx it.

Rita covered her ears, and Alex stared across the scrap of yard, only half listening. They both knew their parents' lines by heart.

"Can't you ever be satisfied?" Dale Beekman demanded. "We've moved almost every year since we got married! Why didn't you just join the Air Force!"

"Because I'm an artist, not a soldier!" Chris Beekman cried. Alex held very still. Dad never raised his voice. This was serious. Their mother said something he couldn't hear. The silence that followed seemed to have its own texture. Finally their father said, very slowly, "Well, if that's the way you feel—"

"Come on." Rita squeezed Alex's hand and looked him in the eye. He nodded, understanding. Time to go in. They stood together and climbed the stairs in tandem. Although they didn't touch, Alex felt attached to his sister as always.

He rapped on the wooden frame and cleared his throat. "Safe to come in?" he called.

Silence. Alex glanced at Rita, then opened the door. Their father sat at the kitchen table, twirling his glasses with one hand. Dale Beekman stood by the sink, filling a glass with water. She turned and gave them a weak smile, but her hand shook and she spilled on the silky dress she'd worn to work. "Hi, kids. How was your day?" she asked.

Alex didn't answer. He circled the table and stopped in front of his father. "Where are we going *this* time?"

Chris Beekman folded his glasses and looked up, blinking as if the room were bright instead of dark and gloomy. Alex bounced on his toes in front of his father. He had that sick, slightly nervous feeling in his stomach that always came to him at the start of a soccer game. He felt Rita's stillness right behind him. Finally their father spoke.

"I had good news today," he said. "One of my scripts sold

to Lorimar Studios. They've asked me to come out to L.A. for a month or two—I may have to rewrite on the spot. If the pilot works out, I might stay on into the fall, do a whole series—and the director is an interesting woman, with all sorts of ties to film. This could be the breakthrough I've been waiting for. But it could also mean four or five months in L.A.—maybe more." He glanced at his wife. "So I was wondering if we should all go back together—at least, for the summer—but apparently your mother doesn't think that's a good idea."

"Los *Angeles?* You're kidding!" Alex couldn't believe it. Something sweet and fizzy rose in his chest, like bubbles drifting upward in champagne.

Chris tried to smile. Without his glasses, his brown eyes seemed small and shy. "I'm sorry," he said suddenly.

"Sorry?" Alex glanced at Rita, expecting her face to show a grin like his own, but she looked pale and frozen, like a store mannequin. Alex was too excited to be puzzled. He circled the table, slamming his fist into his palm. "Back to L.A.— Dad, that's nothing to be sorry about. Hell, it's what I've prayed for every night since we dropped into this stupid town. The question is, how soon can we leave? Tomorrow? My bags are packed."

His father ran his hand over the bald spot on the back of his head. "Let's see—they start casting the end of June. So I guess I'd need to take off in three or four weeks, depending—"

"But that's perfect!" Alex stabbed the calendar on the bulletin board. "In four weeks, school will be out. We can all go together—"

No one said anything. The kitchen suddenly seemed cramped and suffocating. Alex paced up and down in the tiny space near the door. "I don't get it," he said. "Why is this turning into a big crisis? So Dad has to work in L.A. for a few months—is there any reason we can't go along?"

His mother left the sink and sat heavily in a chair, as if

she'd suddenly gained twenty-five pounds. "Alex, in case you haven't noticed, I have a full-time job. Which, by the way, has been paying our bills." She shot her husband a sharp glance. He rubbed his face with one hand, but said nothing. "I can't just walk away from the bank and expect them to take me back." She crossed her arms and turned on her husband. "You promised, when we moved here, that we'd stay until the twins finish high school."

"And what if we don't *want* to finish high school here?" Alex asked.

His mother ignored him. "The fact is, your father's script could turn into a much bigger job. If the series is successful, it could take months to write and produce—am I right?"

"Correct," Chris said, "but there's no way of knowing that now."

"Right. And I'm done with moving. I told you that when we came here, and I meant it. If you go back to L.A., you're on your own."

No one spoke. The refrigerator clicked on, dimming the lights. The fax machine whined and beeped downstairs in the office. The cat stalked across the floor and settled in the tiny pool of sunlight near the door. Everything seemed normal—and yet, it was all too surreal to be believed.

Dale dug into her purse, pulled out a cigarette, and lit it. Alex's mouth fell open. His mother never smoked in the house. "Jesus, Mom, what is this?" he said. "The ultimate screw you to Dad? 'Go to L.A., see if I care?'"

"Don't speak to your mother that way," Chris said in a flat voice.

"It's all right," Dale said, exhaling away from them. "He should be angry."

Her voice was too calm, Alex thought. Like a bomb ticking quietly before it explodes. His mother took a long, deep breath and blew smoke toward the ceiling. "The fact is," she said, "I've had it with being a gypsy. I've done it for eighteen years, and that's enough. Besides—I like it here."

"Mom—are you crazy?" Alex slumped against the wall, letting it hold him up. "This place is *dead*. Nothing happens in Griswold."

"That's right, honey." His mother wiped her smudged mascara with a paper napkin. "*Nothing happens.* No earthquakes, fires, or mud slides. No muggings, freeway shootings, or houses falling onto the Pacific Coast Highway—"

"And no ocean," Alex reminded her. "No paved streets for Rollerblading, no excitement. No music, no galleries, no movie theater with a decent sound system. No one who's a different color or speaks another language. Come on, Mom. I thought you cared about that stuff."

"I do—or at least, I did once," she said. "But you know what? I grew up in a small town. So this feels like home. It's a comfort, knowing everyone."

A comfort? God. Mom had really gone over the edge.

Rita linked her arm through her mother's. "I like it here, too," she said. "I'm just starting to make friends. I don't want to move, either."

Alex stared at Rita. Was this his twin, who always agreed with him? Who saw the world through his own eyes? He felt as if they were on opposite sides of the country already. He struggled to keep his voice steady. "So what are we supposed to do, Mom?"

His mother went to the sink and doused her cigarette. "It's up to you. You could go with your father if you'd like— and come back in the fall. Your grades seem to drop every time you switch schools, but you're seventeen, old enough to make your own decisions."

She's practiced this speech, Alex thought. Practiced the whole damned thing.

"Of course, I assume you'd rather stay where your friends are—"

Alex slammed his fist on the windowsill, rattling the glass. "Friends! Mom, you can't be serious. You think I have friends here?" He stalked to the fridge, grabbed his school picture, and shoved the photo under her nose. "Look at this. Do I look happy?" He didn't let her answer. "Sweet little Alex. Big man on the soccer team. But you know what? The only person who talks to me, in this town, is Molly. Everyone else has decided I'm some kind of weirdo." He lifted his arm, showing her the ragged tear in his shirt. "For example, here's a little present one of my 'friends' gave me today—"

"Alex—" his mother took the photo and reached for him with a ringed hand, but he dodged out of the way. "Sweetheart," she whispered. "Are you having trouble? We didn't know—"

"Well, now you do." Alex stood behind his father's chair. He couldn't look at Rita. He knew his words would tear her apart. "You can't make me stay, Mom. No way. If Dad's leaving, I'm out of here."

His father stood up quickly, knocking his chair over. When he bent to pick it up, he held his back like an old man. "Alex, you're getting too worked up about this. Nothing's carved in stone—and for all I know, I could go to Los Angeles at the end of June, and be home in a month. It's a gamble." He reached in his pocket, pulling out some crumpled dollar bills and the keys to the Honda. "Why don't you kids take off for a while, get a pizza. Give us some time to talk. We'll work something out. We usually do. Right, Dale?"

"It's different this time," their mother said coldly. She turned around and gripped the edge of the sink, her back rigid.

Rita took the keys from her father and went out the door, tears streaming down her face. Alex glanced at his parents, but their faces were grim, and he knew they wouldn't speak again until he was gone. He followed Rita to the car.

"Where to?" Rita asked, turning the key in the ignition. Alex shrugged, but his sister knew where he wanted to go: the only place in town, besides home, where they both felt safe.

"Molly's, then." Rita headed the car down the hill without waiting for Alex to answer.

four

Alex and Rita were quiet as they drove down the hill to River Road. Alex leaned back in his seat, watching the lacy green canopy flash overhead. He'd never lived in a place with such distinct seasons, and he had to admit it was exciting to see everything come alive again. But not as exciting as L.A., he reminded himself.

"You really want to stay here with Mom?" he asked his sister.

"Yes. I do."

"It could be weird," Alex said. "We've never been apart before."

She gave him a quick glance. Her eyes were still sad. "I know. It scares me."

"Why? It's only for the summer."

"I wonder."

Alex took off his dark glasses. "What do you mean?"

"You heard Dad. If the studio likes the pilot, he'll stay longer. You'll probably find Tito—and want to stick around. We could end up with the guys in L.A. and the women at home. That would be a strange family scene."

This was close to the scenario Alex had in his head, except he imagined that somehow, he'd persuade Rita to join him. He wondered if her sixth sense was working on overdrive. "Do you know something I don't know?"

She shook her head. "Not this time. But the way Mom and Dad are talking freaks me out." Her fingers clenched the steering wheel. "What if they don't get back together?" she whispered.

"They will." But of course he was worried about that, too.

Alex closed his eyes, shutting out the dirt road, the clapboard houses set back behind stately sugar maples. In his mind's eye he saw the beach at Bay Street, where Tito taught him to surf. He could smell sunscreen, feel the thick coating of zinc oxide on his nose, hear Hawk, the lifeguard, blow his whistle at some nerdy kid who'd gone out too far. He pictured himself finding Tito, moving in with him when his father came back to Vermont, getting a job, going to school out there, joining his old soccer league . . .

Who was he kidding? Tito might be gone for good. And then what? Alex tried to think of other guys who would be happy to see him, and drew a blank. "You know the best thing about Los Angeles?"

Rita looked annoyed. "Tito and the ocean?"

"Yes, that—but if I didn't find Tito, at least Randy Tovitch wouldn't be there."

Rita didn't answer for a minute. Finally she said, "Alex— there are guys like Randy everywhere. L.A. is full of nasty people."

"So?" Alex guessed what she was getting at, although he didn't feel like hearing it.

"So, it's like what Mom says to Dad all the time, but he doesn't listen: You carry your problems with you."

"I see," Alex said testily. He did *not* like the drift of this conversation one bit. "And what, may I ask, are my problems?"

"You tell me."

He shifted uncomfortably on his seat. Rita was edging much too close to a place he didn't want to go himself. He reached for her hand on the gearshift, but she pulled away. "Rita, listen. Come with me—at least for part of the summer. We'd have a great time."

"That's easy for you to say. I haven't heard from anyone in Los Angeles since we moved. Molly's the first real friend I've had in years." She slowed down for the turn into the

O'Connors' driveway and stopped on the narrow bridge that crossed Rock River, turning to face him. "Alex, you weren't happy in Los Angeles, either. Don't you remember?"

He watched the water rippling away beneath them. Rita was right, as always, but he would never admit it.

The O'Connors' driveway was empty. Good, Alex thought, Todd isn't around. He didn't feel like talking to Molly's older brother. "Wonder if Molly's home?" Alex asked.

"Her bike's here," Rita said. "And it looks like someone else is over, unless Todd's got a new mountain bike—"

Alex looked where she was pointing and sucked in his breath. "You've got to be kidding." As Rita cut the engine, he hopped out of the car and hurried to inspect the mountain bike leaning against the big maple next to Molly's Bianchi. Alex whistled. "Rita, get a load of this." His sister came up behind him. "It's a Barracuda." Alex ran his hand over the two-tone purple frame as if it were a sleek animal. "I checked these out in the catalog, but I've never seen one."

"You guys like my 'Cuda?"

They turned around. The new kid, David Klema, stood on the front porch next to Molly. "This is yours? It's amazing," Alex said.

"Pretty fancy, huh?" Molly called, waving a pair of garden clippers. Alex waved back. Alex envied the way Molly acted. She didn't seem to care what anyone thought of her, and right now she had on a typical Molly outfit: cut-off jeans and a faded T-shirt with holes at the neck. "I'm trying to get Klema to join our team, even though he doesn't have a road bike," she explained as she came down the porch steps. "So, guys, this is David Klema—"

"We met," Alex and Klema said in unison, and smiled awkwardly. As Klema shook hands with Rita, Alex gave him credit for not cruising his sister with his eyes, the way most guys did. But Rita was pretty tall; maybe Klema thought she wouldn't be interested in such a short guy. If so, he'd figured her wrong.

Klema looked at Molly. "I didn't know you were having friends over. Guess I should head home—"

"I didn't know I was having them over, either." Molly winked at Alex, her gray eyes teasing. "Stick around, Mr. Klema. I'm going to cut some lilacs to get rid of the bad smell in the kitchen." Molly tucked her sandy hair behind her ears. "I was just telling Klema about my stepmother, the space cadet. Blair burns dinner, then takes off. Come on, Rita, you can help me."

Alex and Klema watched the girls disappear around the corner of the house. Klema flashed Alex his broad smile. "Want to try the bike?" he asked.

Alex flushed with pleasure. "You don't mind?"

"No—take it down the driveway. The thing rides like a dream."

Alex swung his leg carefully over the frame, settling himself on the seat. "I'm afraid I'll screw it up," he said.

Klema waved him away. "Hell, you can't hurt it. 'Cudas are rugged."

Alex made a few small circles near the barn and then pedaled down the hill. The gears slid and shifted smoothly into place. He bent over the handlebars, cruised across the bridge, and wheeled to a stop, patching out on the gravel. Climbing back to the house, the lowest gear let him pedal easily up the steep hill. He coasted onto the grass and hopped off, setting the bike carefully against the tree, then flopped down near Klema. "It's a beauty. You just buy it?"

"My mom gave it to me. Said she'd get me any bike I wanted, if I'd move here without a fuss. Now I've seen how far we live from everything, I wish I'd asked for a second-hand car—but then I'd have to learn to drive."

"You don't *drive?*"

Klema gave him an embarrassed smile. "No—I'm a true city kid. You don't need a car in Brooklyn. I'll take driver's ed this fall."

He was quiet a minute, and Alex felt awkward, afraid they'd already run out of things to say. But Klema asked, "You do a lot of biking?"

"Yeah. Molly and I are on a bike team—nothing serious; we train together and have unofficial races once a week. You could ride with us."

Klema plucked leaves from the maple tree overhead and rolled them between his fingers. "I'll think about it. I'm not supercompetitive."

"No sweat," Alex said. "Most of us just want to stay in shape for other sports."

"So you're a jock."

Alex shrugged. "Sports are more interesting than school. I like art, too, but there's only one art teacher at the high school."

"Where do you mountain bike?"

"All over." Alex hesitated, afraid of being turned down. But what the hell. There was nothing to lose. He'd be gone in a few weeks anyway. "If you want, I can show you some trails."

Klema surprised him by nodding enthusiastically. "Great," he said. "I'd like that. What do you ride?"

"I use a Bianchi like Molly's for road biking. My mountain bike is an old Specialized; I bought it secondhand when we moved here." Alex glanced behind him. He could hear the girls' voices but couldn't see them. He wished they'd come back. He hadn't realized how much he relied on Rita to make conversation. But Klema didn't seem to have that problem. He kept talking as if they'd known each other a long time.

"What's with Molly? She doesn't look like an athlete—but she's a speed demon. We met on the road, biking home." The gold flecks in Klema's eyes lit up when he smiled. "She didn't even tell me her name—just challenged me to a race up the hill."

Alex grinned. Typical Molly. Few words, plenty of action. "She beat you?"

"Yeah—by a lot. Embarrassing. Especially since I've got this bike that's supposed to let me ride like a bandit."

"Molly's fast," Alex said. "She's into biathlon."

Klema squinted, his dark eyebrows pulled into a straight line. "What's that?"

"A crazy sport where you cross country ski and shoot."

"Oh, right. I've seen it on TV. Girls do that?"

"Yeah. Molly worked hard to convince her dad it was okay to use a gun."

Klema laughed. "That would go over big in Brooklyn, if we ever had enough snow. Self-defense on skis."

Alex leaned against the trunk of the tree. This guy was so easy to talk to—how long since he'd felt that way? Since Tito, of course. His gaze wandered down the hill and out to the low mountains on the other side of the river. Damn Tito, anyway. Everything Alex did and thought about circled around to him.

Molly and Rita came back around the corner of the house, their arms filled with deep blue lilacs the color of Rita's eyes. Rita buried her face in the blooms, then held them under Alex's nose. "Remind you of anything?" she asked.

He sniffed quickly and shook his head. Then something came back, a vague memory of a bush near a door . . . where was it? "Oregon?" he asked.

"Our little house in Portland." Rita's eyes filled, and she ducked her nose into the flowers again until she was calm. Alex looked away. For a few minutes, talking to Klema, he'd managed to forget the scene at home. Now his knee twitched as if someone were hitting his reflex point with a rubber hammer. He wondered if Rita had told Molly what was going on.

No one spoke for a minute, and things felt awkward. Finally Molly said, "So—you want something to eat?"

They went inside. Alex sniffed. "Geez—it smells like burned rubber in here. What was she cooking?"

"Rice, probably. Let's hope we don't have to eat it tonight." Molly stuck one bunch of lilacs into a tall jug, wrapped the other in wet towels for Rita to take home, then gave out sodas and opened a bag of chips. They followed her back to the porch. Alex and Klema sat on the steps, while the girls perched on the railing above them. Molly looked at Rita, then Alex. "So what's up?" she asked. "You're awful quiet."

Good old Molly. Straight to the point. Alex glanced at Rita, who shrugged. *Go ahead,* she seemed to say. *You tell her.* "We had an upset at home," Alex explained. "Dad has a job in L.A. for the summer—and I think I'll go with him." He glanced at his sister. "Mom and Rita might stay here."

"What do you mean, *might*?" Rita rubbed her bare arms as if she were cold. "Mom and I are clear—we won't budge."

Molly set her drink under the porch swing. "I'd *pay* my dad to take Todd away for the summer." She watched them carefully, her eyes narrowing. "Guess you guys don't like being apart, though."

"It's not that." Rita hesitated and glanced at Klema, biting her lip. Alex knew she was about to cry, and Klema must have figured that out, too, because he stood up suddenly, his eyes wary. "Maybe I should take off."

"That's okay," Rita said, but her voice shook and she turned away.

Molly nudged her. "Come on, let's talk upstairs. Excuse us, guys."

Alex watched them go in. Why was Rita so upset about all this? After all, it wasn't a divorce—was it?

Klema set his soda on the porch and studied Alex. "Back to L.A. Just what you wanted, right? You must be psyched."

"I guess," Alex said. "Like you said about your situation, it's complicated."

"Sorry." Klema sounded as if he meant it. He started toward his bike. "So—see you tomorrow?"

"Wait," Alex said quickly. He didn't want to be stuck alone with his worries. "I'll show you the river. If you'd like," he added, giving Klema the chance to shoot him down. But Klema looked pleased. "Sure," he said, and followed Alex through the pasture.

"Watch the fence," Alex warned, swinging his leg high over the woven wire. "It gives a nasty shock."

He led Klema down the hill, ducking under the white pine branches onto the path he and Molly took when they wanted to talk. The stream was still full from spring rains. Alex always felt relaxed the minute he heard Rock River's steady rippling sound. It reminded him of early mornings on the coast, when the Pacific was calm and the beach empty.

Alex cut down the steep bank and stepped onto a flat boulder near the water. Klema stood beside him, watching the tiny waves ripple past a small grassy island, then leaned over to pick up some heavy stones. He set them in a line near the bank and glanced at Alex, the gold lights flickering in his eyes. "Are we too old to build a dam?" he asked.

"No way." Alex took off his shoes. So far, his first impression was right on. Klema was a good guy.

They gathered big stones from the bank and rolled them into the water, grunting and puffing.

"You and Rita twins?" Klema asked Alex, after they'd set their first row of stones in the deep water.

"Yeah."

"You look alike," he said, and grinned. "Lucky for you, huh?"

So Klema *had* noticed his sister. Alex wasn't sure how to respond to the compliment, but Klema didn't seem to expect an answer; he went right on talking. "You're going to L.A. no matter what?"

"If my dad will take me." For a stranger, the guy sure asked direct questions. "It would be weird, though. Rita and I have always been together."

"Sometimes I wish I had a brother or sister," Klema said, "but my friends who have them fight all the time, so maybe I shouldn't complain. Still, it's hard going through tough family stuff alone." He stepped out onto a smooth rock, extending the dam with bigger stones. "You and Rita ever fight?"

Alex rolled a big hunk of white quartz into the water. "Not much. We've always been close. It's funny—our parents go out of their way to point out how different we are. They keep us in separate classes at school. It's almost like they *want* us to fight and be jealous, like ordinary brothers and sisters." Alex picked up a big stone and set it on the end of the dam.

Klema grunted, setting a heavy boulder in place. "Can you talk to her about anything?"

"Just about." Alex was tempted to tell him how Rita could sometimes dart right into his mind to read his thoughts, but he held back. Klema might think that was weird.

"Man, you're lucky. Maybe you'd better stick together," Klema said.

"Yeah. We'll see what happens." Alex wondered how his voice could stay so flat when his insides felt like whirlpools surging around his feet, turning back on themselves and roiling downstream. What was causing those feelings? Fear? The worry that something horrible had happened to Tito? Shove that idea, Beekman. He stepped into the cold water, piling stones onto the dam.

Klema went upstream, tucked a big stone under each arm, and brought them back to the river. Alex carted rocks from the shore out into the middle of the stream. Klema winced whenever he stepped into the water. "Jesus!" he cried. "Feels like the ice just melted."

Alex laughed. "It did."

They were quiet for a while, moving rocks until their shirts stuck to their backs and their foreheads glistened with sweat. The water slowed and deepened a little behind their wall of glossy stones. They kept at it until the dam stretched across the small channel, then waded back to shore and sat in the sun to warm their feet. "Next time, we'll dam the whole river," Klema said.

Alex smiled. "Yeah." He felt good; satisfied, in fact. Hell, it was only a dam, a line of rocks, but he felt as if he'd accomplished something for once. Plus, *doing* something with a guy was usually easier than talking. He'd certainly learned that with Tito.

Klema cupped water in his hands and wet his curly hair, slicking it back with his fingers. "It's nice here, you know?" His waving hand took in the river, their dam, the sunlight sparkling on the pool they'd created. "Nothing like this in Brooklyn, that's for sure." He laughed. "It's so quiet here at night, I can't sleep. Strange, huh?"

"I know. I remember when we first came, I missed the sound of traffic." Alex flicked a stone into the water. "No rivers in L.A. either, unless you count the ones that flow in concrete riverbeds. But there's ocean. And things happening."

"You wouldn't miss Molly?"

Alex glanced at him. "Sure. But she's not my girlfriend, if that's what you mean."

"You could do worse," Klema said with a smile. "Still, if you stayed—" he began, then stopped.

Alex looked into Klema's eyes, which were bright with mischief. "What?" he asked.

"You said Griswold was dead. Maybe we could make something happen here. Liven things up. With Rita and Molly—and there's a brother, too, right? What's Todd like?"

"He's okay," Alex said. This was too much. Finally, someone in Griswold he could talk to—just when he was leaving? Maybe he was nuts. But then he thought of the scene in the locker room, and heard Mrs. Perone saying, *Tito doesn't live here anymore.* He had no choice.

Alex didn't know Klema well enough to explain why he had to leave. Instead, he watched the water licking their new dam. He'd run out of things to say.

Klema cleared his throat and checked his watch. "I'd better split. My mom will be pacing—she still has city nerves."

They put on their shoes and climbed back up the driveway. As Klema picked up his bike he asked, "So—want to show me some bike trails sometime?"

"Sure," Alex said. "There are some good ones near my place."

"I'll call you," Klema said. "It's Beekman, right? You in the book?"

"New listings," Alex said with a tight smile. "We never have the same number too long."

"That's a drag." Klema slung a pack over his shoulder and climbed on his bike. "Tell Molly good-bye for me, will you?"

"Sure. Take it easy." Alex watched Klema wheel down the driveway, bent over the flashing purple frame as if he were hugging it in his arms. Alex sighed. At last, a decent guy who might want to be his friend. If it weren't for Tovitch—

Alex kicked a stone into the field. So what? Even if Tovitch turned Klema against him, he'd be out of here in four weeks. Gone. To a place so far away, even Tovitch couldn't touch him.

five

When Molly said good-bye to Alex, her thin face
was pinched. "I'm afraid if you leave, you'll never come back."

"Don't worry. Anyway, it's not for another month. We still
have lots of time together." Alex avoided Molly's eyes. He'd
been complaining about Griswold from the minute his family
first drove down the town's run-down main street last summer.
So why this sudden sharp pain in his gut, now that he could
finally split?

"I'll miss you," Molly said, and pulled him into a tight hug,
surprising them both. Her wiry back softened under Alex's
hands, and two bright pink spots pulsed on her cheeks when
she pulled away. "I just invited Rita to be a partner in my lawn-
mowing business. You could work with us, if you stay."

Alex shook his head. "No way. I can't tell a weed from a
rosebush." He squeezed her shoulder. "But thanks for asking."
He climbed into the car.

Molly leaned into his open window. "Call tonight. Let me
know what's happening."

"We will."

Dinner that night was strained. Their parents chatted about
movies and work as if nothing important had happened all day.
Rita picked at her food, and finally pushed back her plate, saying, "Okay, what's going on?"

Their parents exchanged awkward looks. Chris Beekman
cleared his throat. "I'm going to Los Angeles at the end of June.
The studio found me a furnished sublet off Rose Avenue in

Venice. Anyone who wants to come with me is welcome." He looked around the table, his small eyes resting nervously on each of them.

"Rose Avenue?" Alex asked. "That's right near the board-walk, isn't it? Five minutes to the beach. I'm coming."

Silence. Alex glanced nervously at his sister, waiting.

"I'm staying," Rita said at last. Her lip trembled, and she turned away.

They looked at their mother. "You already know my plans," she said, and went outside for her after-dinner ciga-rette.

Just like that—it was settled. Alex couldn't believe it. He jumped up to help his father clear the table and wash up. Rita went upstairs to play the flute, and soon a mournful tune drifted down the stairs. Her music always told the family how she was feeling.

As Alex dried the dishes, his father asked, "Got any plans tonight?"

Alex stiffened inside. His father couldn't get off this track lately. "Not really. Just hanging out here. I'm tired."

Chris scrubbed the big pasta pot. "Why don't you take that nice Molly O'Connor to a movie?"

Alex looked down on his father. The bald spot on the back of his dad's head was shiny under the light, and his jowled cheeks seemed to sag. Chris was definitely looking older and more shrunken these days. So how could he still make Alex feel so bad? "In the first place, 'that nice Molly' is busy tonight—helping Blair hang a show of her work at the gallery," Alex said, angrily stacking the plates in the cup-board over the stove. "We do go to the movies sometimes, but she's just a friend. How come you're so intense about this, Dad? Rita doesn't have a date tonight, but I don't see you bugging *her*."

"True." His father looked away, embarrassed. "It just

seems like you don't make much of an effort to fit in here."

"Fitting in means having a girlfriend?"

"That's not what I meant—"

"Well, that's how it sounds. Give me a break, will you?" Alex threw the dish towel over the hook and went into the bathroom, slamming the door behind him. He didn't have to pee, but sometimes the bathroom was the only place to escape. He closed the lid of the toilet and sat with his head in his hands. Why did he get so bent out of shape when his father bugged him this way? Lots of other juniors weren't dating, although they strutted around, boasting that they couldn't keep the chicks away.

Truth was, right now he didn't want a girlfriend. Was that so bad?

Maybe he should pretend to have a crush on Molly. Alex laughed to himself. He wouldn't get far with that one. Molly could spot a phony a mile away.

When Alex heard his father go downstairs, he flushed the toilet and went outside. His mother leaned on the porch railing, a cigarette dangling from her right hand. She gazed off into the trees and something about her dreamy expression reminded Alex of Rita. But Dale's face was a chalky gray in the slanting sunlight, and her dyed blond hair seemed too young for her face. Alex had a sudden vision of what he and his sister might look like in thirty years. It spooked him.

Dale turned around. "Come here," she said, "I want to show you something." She ground her finished cigarette under her heel and pointed at the woods. "The shad is in bloom."

Alex followed the line of her hand. Filmy white blossoms speckled the woods like powdered sugar. "I thought spring would never come," she said.

"If we lived in L.A., you wouldn't have to wait for spring," Alex said, and then immediately felt guilty when he saw the sadness in her face. "I'm sorry, Mom. I never thought you would like it here."

She cupped her hand over his. "Neither did I. I surprised myself." Her blue eyes searched his face. "Alex, I know you'd like to move back. But what if I pick up again, quit my job—and your father's deal falls through? We could be right where we started last fall—living in a house we can't afford, with your schooling disrupted again. I know I'm doing the right thing, although you and your father must think I'm being stubborn."

"It's all right, Mom. Really."

She ruffled his hair softly, the way she used to when he was little. "Thanks," she said. "I'll miss you, you know. Don't stay too long."

Alex let her hug him, but he didn't answer. He had already promised himself he wouldn't come back until he'd found Tito—and he certainly couldn't tell her that. He took a deep breath, pulling away gently. "What will you do if the studio wants Dad to stick around?"

It took her a long time to answer; much too long. Finally she said, "Don't worry about that now. It's a long way off. Who knows how we'll all feel at the end of the summer."

Not a very comforting response. But at least she didn't talk about divorce. His parents weren't tight, Alex realized, and maybe they never had been. They didn't do much together, but they didn't fight a lot, either. Were they happy? No way he'd ask his mother *that* question. He wasn't ready to hear the answer. Alex swatted at the clouds of blackflies gathering in the dusk.

Rita's flute trilled upstairs, then sank to a sweet, haunting melody. "I wish you'd take Rita with you," Dale said. "I worry about you two being apart."

Alex leaned on the railing beside her. "We'll have to get used to it someday," he said. "Might as well start practicing now." He sounded just like his mother—putting a fake smile on everything. But he didn't feel that cocky inside.

"It's lonely, moving all the time," Dale said softly. "You can't imagine how lonely it is."

Alex turned away, his eyes stinging. She should try living inside *his* head, if she wanted to know about lonely.

Alex's mother shook him awake early the next morning, handing him the portable phone. "Your friend's on the line," she said.

Alex rolled over with a groan, ready to give Molly hell for waking him so early on a Saturday, but the deep voice on the other end took him by surprise. It was Klema.

"Damn, Beekman—I'm sorry. I told your mother not to wake you."

Alex stifled a yawn and hunched his shoulders to stretch them. "'S'all right. What's up?"

"Look outside. It's a great day for biking. I was hoping you could show me those trails." Klema lowered his voice. "Otherwise, I'll get stuck doing yard work for my mom."

"Sure," Alex said sleepily. "Come on over." He gave Klema directions and then swung his legs to the side, forcing himself out from under the covers. Strike one against Klema, he thought. Much too cheerful in the morning. But Alex couldn't stop smiling.

Alex took a quick shower to clear the fuzz from his head, and was eating a second waffle when Klema coasted into the driveway. The Beekmans practically fell all over themselves greeting Klema, until Alex wanted to stuff socks in their mouths. Did his parents have to make it so obvious that he didn't have friends in this town?

Alex filled his water bottle and hustled Klema out the door. They biked without saying much, climbing to the top of

Soldier's Hill where Alex turned into the woods, following a network of old logging trails that Molly had showed him last fall. Before long, they were sweaty and hot; they stopped to tie their sweatshirts around their waists, then took off again. Alex led the way, standing up in his lowest gear as his tires churned deep into the litter of wet leaves. Mud sprayed up onto the back of his shirt and shorts; it felt good to work hard. After a few miles, they stopped to rest, and clouds of blackflies swarmed around their heads.

"Damn!" Klema said, cinching his helmet tighter under his chin. "What are these buggers?"

"Blackflies," Alex said. "Part of the idyllic country life. They come out when it gets warm, and they love sweat. Miserable, huh?" He mashed one on his arm; his fingertips came away bloody.

"Another strike against Vermont," Klema said.

Alex nodded. "You're not kidding. Even the locals complain about blackfly season." He waved his hands in front of his face, trying to shoo the bugs away. "Take that next trail to the right and loop back to the road; it's better in the open."

Klema took the lead this time, and Alex enjoyed watching him from behind. From this angle, he could be a short version of Tito. His legs were just as powerful, and his back had that same wide, muscular look Alex always envied. But Klema didn't have Tito's energy. Following Tito in any sport— skating, surfing, biking—always left Alex feeling breathless, but Klema was panting hard by the time they rejoined Soldier's Hill Road. Alex was only slightly winded, which made him feel secretly pleased. His long bike rides with Molly had paid off.

They turned right and cruised downhill, heads bent over their handlebars. Suddenly, Klema yelled, "Watch it!"

A truck hurtled toward them, horn blaring. Alex swerved off the road, hit the ditch, and fell off sideways, scraping his

right leg in the gravel. "Damn!" He somersaulted out of the
way as Klema dodged the truck, tangled with a long stick lying
in the road, and went flying into the tall grass. "Son of a
bitch!" Alex cried. "Goddamn, Tovitch." The truck screeched
to a halt, and the transmission whined as Randy rammed it
into reverse.

Alex picked himself up slowly and wrestled his bike back
onto the road. Klema bent over his 'Cuda. "Asshole broke my
chain. Is this the guy you warned me about yesterday?"

"The very one." Alex's head throbbed and his leg burned,
but he refused to look down. Inspecting his wounds would
only give Tovitch more ammunition.

The truck rocked to a halt beside them, and Randy leaned
out the window. "Well, well. If it isn't Mutt and Jeff," he said
with a nasty grin. "So sorry I ruined your little bike ride."

"Yeah, right." Alex unsnapped his helmet, pushing his
sweaty hair off his forehead. "I bet you're *real* sorry."

"Going kind of fast, weren't you?" Klema said.

Tovitch raised his hands. "Guilty, officer," he said, flashing
his chipped-tooth smile at Klema—who didn't smile back.

"Lucky you didn't kill us." Klema's face was a deep, cop-
pery red.

Randy frowned. "Listen, I said sorry. And it doesn't look
like any serious damage was done—except for your sweetie's
leg," he said, pointing at Alex.

Alex couldn't speak, but Klema was obviously too angry to
notice. "I've got a broken chain," he told Tovitch. When
Randy didn't respond, Klema added, "I'll let you know how
much it costs."

Tovitch leaned forward, checking out the bike. "A brand-
new 'Cuda. Aren't you the lucky one. We can't afford bikes
like that around here. Let me know what it costs to fix it." He
laughed. "Of course, there's no way I'll give you the money."
He leered at Alex. "This your new *girlfriend,* Beekman?"

Alex wanted to fling his helmet in Randy's face, but he still couldn't move. He hated himself for being this way, hated it when his brain shut down like a computer whose screen suddenly goes blank.

Klema turned and looked behind him, carefully and slowly. "No girls in sight," he said, his voice controlled and quiet.

Randy shifted into neutral and revved the engine. "Hey, no harm meant. But if I were new in town, I wouldn't pick the local fag as my first friend, know what I mean? I suppose a runt like you likes to hang out with the big guys—but who knows what queer virus runs in those veins—"

Klema's body exploded. He jumped onto the truck's running board and gripped the window frame with both hands, bristling all over. "Watch your language," he said fiercely.

Randy's grin looked pasted on. "Hoping for a fight, shrimp?"

"I *said*, watch your language." Klema leaned into the cab, his helmet nearly touching Randy's forehead. "And yes, I'd love a fight. I haven't had a good match since the day I won my black belt. It would be a pleasure, trying some karate kicks on you." He jumped down from the truck, yanking the door open. "Get down."

Randy reached out, grabbed the door, and pulled it shut. "Take it easy, guy. Just offering a little friendly advice—"

"I can choose my friends without your help," Klema said, his voice still tight. "And if you come after me with your gang of thugs, I'll be ready. We know how to fight in Brooklyn."

"My, my." Tovitch tried to sound casual, but Alex noticed he locked the door with his elbow. "Mister short guy has to prove he's tough." Randy rammed the truck into gear. "But hey, I'm cool. Now, move it."

"My pleasure." Klema stepped aside, and Tovitch pealed off down the hill.

Klema stood in the middle of the road, his legs planted far

apart, until the truck disappeared around the corner, while Alex jumped the ditch and sat on the bank, inspecting his leg. He was ashamed to look Klema in the eye. Klema had said he could choose his own friends—but who would want to hang out with a total wimp? Especially someone with a black belt. At least Klema had stood up for himself. Alex hadn't even opened his mouth. He had run circles around Tovitch on the soccer field last fall. Why was he such a coward now?

Klema unsnapped his helmet, tossed it into the grass, and bent over his bike, wrestling the stick from the chain. "Shit," he said. "I can't believe I let that asshole get to me."

"He's hard to ignore." Alex picked stones from his cut, wincing. The scrape stung like crazy now; a long, rutted, and ugly wound pocked with gravel.

Klema leaned over to take a look, and whistled. "Nasty."

"Yeah. A true raspberry." Alex stood up. "Sorry I screwed up your weekend—not to mention your 'Cuda—"

"Hey, it's not your fault." Klema rubbed gravel over his palms to cut the grease from his chain. "What's Randy's problem, anyway?"

"Who knows? His father is a jerk. My sister thinks he beats Randy up." Alex decided not to mention Rita's newest theory about Randy's behavior.

"He acts like someone who's been pushed around," Klema said, "but that's no excuse."

They lifted their bikes over the ditch and walked down the road without talking. Alex watched a stuck pebble circle around in his front tire. Klema was still breathing hard beside him. A half mile down the road, Klema stopped short and swore under his breath. "I'm still so pumped up—I can't believe I broke my karate teacher's most important rule."

"Which is?"

"Don't ever let the enemy see your Achilles' heel."

Alex glanced down at him. "What do you mean?"

"Didn't you see how I lost it when he called me a runt? If I'd been smart, I would have ignored him. It's not like I haven't heard *that* before." He smiled, but his eyes stayed hard. "Now he knows how to jerk my chain. Yours, too. He gets his kicks by calling you a fag, right?" he said.

Alex's gut tightened. "Apparently."

Klema looked up at him. "Who cares? You told me yourself Tovitch carries a grudge. Why does it push your buttons?"

Alex gripped his handlebars. Klema wasn't as smart as he'd thought. "What are you getting at?"

Klema cocked his head. "Easy, man. I'm not saying you're *gay*. I just wondered—"

"Yeah, well you can quit wondering." Alex tried to keep his voice calm, but his Adam's apple seemed to be stuck in his throat. "And you can keep your friendly theories to yourself." Alex swung his leg over his bike, tucked his head, and pedaled furiously down the hill, his eyes burning hot as the scrape on his leg.

"Beekman!" Klema shouted, but Alex skidded around the corner and kept going, his head tucked into the wind. Now he'd done it. Let his own screwed-up head ruin everything. Burned his last bridge in this nowhere town.

SIX

Alex glanced nervously around the caf before he went in on Monday. The place was a madhouse, but there was no sign of Tovitch. Alex didn't dare let his guard down; he was poised to bolt as he stood in line at the soda machine, and he jumped when he felt a tap on his shoulder.

"Easy, man." Alex whirled to see Klema looking up at him with a shy smile. Alex didn't know what to say. Since Saturday, he'd assumed Klema was a nonfriend, out of the picture like so many other guys in Griswold. Klema rescued him. "Listen, I'm sorry about the other day. There's something I need to explain. Meet me later?"

Alex shoved change into the soda machine and waited for his drink to rumble into the bin. "I've got a big art project due this week—"

"No sweat," Klema said. "This won't take long. You have bike team after school?"

"Not today," Alex said.

"Meet me at the bike racks, then." Klema gave him a gentle punch on the arm. "And lighten up, Beekman. Your shoulders are up to your ears."

Alex tossed his hair off his forehead and tried to relax. It was hard to stay mad at this guy. "You got your 'Cuda fixed?"

"Right away. Sent the bill to Tovitch, as promised." Klema raised his hand. "I'm late for class. Ciao."

Alex popped his soda open and watched Klema navigate the noisy room, cruising between huddles of students as if he were on a crowded city street. His black clothes, black high-tops, and slicked-back hair made him look out of place, but unlike Alex, Klema obviously didn't care about that stuff. And the guy had guts, sending Tovitch a bill. He'd been that cocky once, Alex thought. When had he lost it?

That was easy to answer. When he left L.A.—and Tito.

Drop it, Beekman, he told himself. You've got Tito on the brain. He hurried down the hall to the empty art room, his only safe haven during lunch hour.

At three o'clock, Klema was waiting at the bike rack, his backpack slung over one shoulder. He grinned at Alex as if nothing had gone wrong between them. "So where do you go if you want a cappuccino in this town?"

"You kidding? Coffee bars haven't hit Griswold yet. But there's a bagel place on Main Street—they have good straight coffee, and tables outside."

"Sounds good. I'll buy."

Alex forgot his excuse about needing to do homework. He was ravenous after skipping lunch. He and Klema biked down Main Street and locked their bikes to a lamppost outside the restaurant. They went through the main room to the deck overlooking Rock River. The spray from the stream made the air chilly; the tables were empty, but Klema took one near the railing, farthest from the door. Alex pulled on his sweatshirt, and Klema took a jacket from his pack. "We'll pretend it's spring," he said, huddling into the leather. They ordered coffee and garlic bagels, and Alex watched the gray-green rapids surge past, each wave licking a brown boulder in a different rhythm, the light shifting and flickering under the footbridge.

"Earth to Beekman."

Alex swung around. "Sorry. I was just thinking how hard it is to draw light on water."

"Hey, I'm impressed you can draw anything. What's your art project?"

"A collage, with sea turtles. I'll show you sometime." The waitress brought coffee; Alex loaded it with cream and sugar and asked quickly, to get it over with, "So what did you need to tell me?"

Klema blew on his coffee, then cradled the mug in his hands. "I didn't mean to put you on the spot the other day." Klema glanced around, but the deck was still empty. He kept his voice low. "I know you're not gay. That's obvious."

Alex's hand shook. He set his coffee down. "Gee, thanks."

Klema leaned back in his chair. "As they say in New York, chill out, man." He smiled. "Look, I was trying to talk about attitude. You saw what happened to me. Tovitch calls me a runt, and I blow it; hold up a flag saying 'Here's my weak spot. Go for it!' " Klema socked himself in the gut.

Alex smiled. Damn. He did like this guy.

Klema sipped his coffee. "I guess I was talking to myself as much as to you. It's basic first-grade stuff. If you stay cool when the class bully calls you names, eventually, he might leave you alone. Right?"

"My sister tells me the same thing," Alex admitted. "That's why I keep my mouth shut."

"Right. But fear is written all over your face. Hell, I'm a fine one to talk. But maybe if we stick together, we can help each other. Deal?" Klema reached across the table.

Alex gave him a weak smile as they shook hands. "Sure." But he knew, from experience, that nothing could stop Tovitch once he got started. Klema would find that out soon enough.

The waitress kicked the door open and brought out their plates. Alex lathered the warm bagel with cream cheese and took a bite. His leg was twitching under the table; he was eager to change the subject. "When did you start karate?" he asked.

"Junior high. I was always the class runt, but my voice

changed when I was twelve. I got a mustache and shot up a few inches—thought I had it made. But that was the end of my growth spurt. The rest of the guys just kept passing me by. Shooting up like basketball stars." He grinned at Alex. "Like you, in fact. What are you, six two?"

"Something like that." Although he was taller, Alex didn't want to rub it in. The waitress poured more coffee, and Alex cradled the mug to warm his hands.

"Anyway, I was sick of being picked on," Klema said. "Guns and knives scare me, so martial arts seemed like the best way to protect myself."

Alex shook his head in disbelief. Even though Klema was short, the guy's broad shoulders, cocky stance, and cheeks darkened by the bluish tinge of a beard did *not* make him seem like the type to get cornered in the school yard. "You going to keep up the karate here?"

"If I can find a dojo. I'm still at the lowest dan of black belt, and I'd like to go on. Want to join me?"

Alex hesitated. "Maybe."

"Hey, no pressure. Just asking." They finished their bagels in silence. At the cash register, Klema asked, "Still planning on going to the Coast?"

Alex nodded, and as they wheeled their bikes along the sidewalk he decided Klema seemed safe. "I'm not just getting away from Vermont. My best buddy in L.A. disappeared."

Klema stopped, his helmet dangling from his wrist. "Rough. You mean like a kidnapping or something?"

"No, but it's pretty weird. His parents kicked him out of the house, and his mother wouldn't tell me why. She practically spit at me through the phone. Claims she doesn't know where he is. Someplace in L.A. Man—it takes hours even to fly over that city, it's so huge. I don't know how I'd ever find him—"

"But you have to try."

"Right." Alex smiled, relieved. Klema seemed to understand better than his own sister. They wheeled their bikes to the corner and stood waiting for the light to change.

"You think your friend did something violent?" Klema asked.

"He's not the type. But he's a wild guy, so Rita thinks he could have pulled one crazy stunt too many. He talked about buying a motorcycle, which could have freaked his parents out—they're pretty conservative, but not enough to send him away. Anyway, that's why I'm outta here."

"For sure. Too bad I can't come along—we could track him down together. Form a detective agency for missing persons."

Alex stared at him. The guy was serious. Amazing. Without even thinking of the consequences, Alex said, "Want me to ask my dad? He might not mind."

"Thanks. My mom would have a fit. Her leash is long and flexible, but she likes to be able to reel me in. She'll be in a state of shock when I go to college." Klema clipped his helmet on. "I'm a chess player. I like to figure out a guy's next move before he even sees it himself. Finding someone might be like a chess match. You'd think: Where would he go next? And why? How can I get there before he does? You can call me from L.A. this summer to try out your theories. Hell, I'm going to need something to occupy my brain."

"Thanks," Alex said. "I might just do that."

At the end of the street, they bumped their bikes off the curb and pedaled slowly out of town, picking up the pace as they left the traffic behind and turned onto Soldier's Hill Road. Alex tucked down over his handlebars, and Klema imitated him, pedaling fast to keep up. Alex grinned, pumping harder. Klema increased the pace; so did Alex. Neither of them said anything, but it suddenly became an unspoken race to Klema's turn. Klema dropped behind on the flat, but when the pavement ended and the hill began, Alex heard his heavy breathing come up behind him. He pushed until his lungs burned, shooting ahead one length just before they reached River Road.

Alex braked, swerved to the side near the river, and straddled his bike. "Thought you said you weren't competitive," he said, teasing, when he could finally talk.

Klema bent over the handlebars, his face mottled from the exercise. "Oh, yeah. I forgot."

Alex took a long hit from his water bottle, then passed it over to Klema, who smiled and drank, then squirted water over his face. "Do this again?" Klema asked.

Alex wasn't sure if Klema meant the bike race, or going out for coffee, but he was game for either. "Definitely." He glanced at his watch. "Guess I'd better go, or I'll be in trouble with my art project. Thanks for the bagel."

"No problem. And I enjoyed the ride the other day," Klema said, "in spite of Tovitch." He slapped Alex's shoulder. "Adios."

"See you." Alex turned and started up the hill, glancing behind him as he rounded the corner. Klema looked small and lost, standing alone at the crossroads, but his face brightened when Alex waved and he tossed him a thumbs-up as he took off.

Klema was an interesting guy, Alex thought. A cool guy, in fact. For a second, he wondered if he was doing the right thing, taking off on a search for one friend who'd disappeared, when it seemed like he had a new one waiting. As his fingers curled around his handlebars Alex glanced at the silver ring on his hand. If *he* disappeared, Tito would come looking for him, wouldn't he? Of course he would. That's what friends were for.

"Four more weeks, Perone," he said. "And then—I'm coming after you."

PART TWO

SUMMER

LOS ANGELES, CALIFORNIA

I'm riding behind Tito on his new motorcycle. The cold wind rushes past us. I grip his waist and tuck my head against his shoulder, pressing my chest against his broad back as we speed through Los Angeles. The engine whines. We book it down crowded city streets, weaving through traffic, running red lights. I scream at Tito to slow down, but he laughs and leans forward into the wind, pulling me with him.

We squeal around a corner and fishtail to a sudden stop. Tito jumps from the bike. I tumble after him, running to keep up. He scales a chain-link fence; I follow, catching my pants on the jagged wire as I fling myself over the top. I fall as I land, and when I scramble to my feet, I see we're at La Brea.

Tito runs to the far side of the tar pit and beckons to me, his dark eyes gleaming like the oil oozing up from under the ground. I look down into the pit, where mastodons and saber-toothed tigers lie encased in oil, caught forever in the thick tar. The pit pulsates. A hoof emerges from the oil, then disappears. An antelope rears her head, dark eyes frantic, as tar coats her flaring nostrils. I watch, horrified, yet unable to move.

Tito calls my name. He stands on the far side of the pit, holding out his hands. I start toward him, but La Brea is expanding, throbbing with life like an overturned anthill. Hot tar bubbles up and spreads onto the city streets, licking my feet.

Tito calls me again, his voice hoarse, urgent. I look into the pit and understand: To reach Tito, I have to swim across. I hesitate on the edge when suddenly, someone shoves me from behind. I lose my footing on the slick rim and slide down into the oil, holding my breath as the tar sucks me in and covers my eyes, smothering me. . . .

seven

"**Alex,   wake   up.** Wake up! You're having a dream."

Alex woke with a start, his teeth clenched, his sleeping bag tangled around him. His father's whisper seemed loud in the silence of the campground. Alex swallowed a groan and rolled over on his stomach. He was hard, and drenched in cold sweat.

His father slithered from his sleeping bag, unzipped the tent, and stumbled a few feet into the woods to pee. Alex took a deep breath. Of all his nightmares, this was the worst yet. What the hell did it mean?

He shifted on his foam pad, trying to avoid a twisted root under his hips. They'd made pretty good time since they left Vermont, settling into a routine of three-hour shifts at the wheel. Crossing Nebraska drove him crazy. It went on forever: flat cropland bristling with new green corn, nothing to break the monotony of the wheels turning. Dad hardly spoke, just hummed to himself, usually some tune that didn't match whatever was playing on the tape deck, which drove Alex crazy. And then his father decided to take the scenic route through the Rockies, which cut down on their speed. Alex drove too fast during his shifts; he just wanted to get there.

They had crossed the New Mexico border after dark, passing dramatic silver cliffs that deepened to a rosy pink at sunset. "We're in Georgia O'Keeffe territory," his father told him, but Alex was too nervous to think about one of his favorite artists; he had to concentrate on the wild animals that came flying across the highway at dusk. They seemed to be taking part in some weird kamikaze routine. An elk loomed out of the sagebrush and stumbled in front of them, just missing the bumper. Mule deer leaped onto the asphalt in pairs, and the carcasses of animals who hadn't made it lay humped up on the narrow shoulders of the pavement.

By the time they finally pulled over, somewhere outside of Santa Fe, Alex had to pry his fingers from the steering wheel, and his eyes ached from the tension of watching the road. His stomach gnawed; Dad was happy to snack on stuff from the cooler, but Alex felt as if he hadn't eaten a real meal since they left home.

Now Chris Beekman crouched in front of the tent, unzipped it, and crawled inside, wriggling into his bag. "Okay?" he asked Alex.

"Yeah," Alex murmured, trying to sound sleepy. In fact, he was wide awake. His heart was thumping, maybe from the altitude; he had a tight headache right behind his eyes. He lay still, listening to the wind swish like water through the ponderosas. A tiny animal scrabbled on the roof of the tent, under the fly; even though Alex knew it was outside, it made him nervous. He slapped the tight nylon, and the animal slid off with a high "chirrup, chirrup." Chris Beekman was oblivious; he breathed slow and deep. Alex felt trapped sleeping so close to his father in the tent he'd shared with Rita on all their moves and camping trips.

Damn. He couldn't get Rita out of his mind; the accusing look in her eyes that had haunted him ever since he left Vermont. "Hey, it won't be long," he'd said when he left because, in the end, she'd decided to visit them in August, if they were still there.

As for his mother—that was even worse. Dale almost acted as if she were glad they were leaving. She kept talking about "us girls" having the house to themselves—as if Alex and his dad wouldn't be welcome when they came back.

If they came back. Of course, Klema and Molly were both counting on seeing him in time for soccer practice in August. Alex had kept his secret tucked inside: If Tito had a place of his own, Alex might try to stay. Trouble was, Rita had psyched him out. She never said it, but she must have had a hunch about his plan because she played bluesy songs of loss on her flute until the house seemed morbid.

Only Klema understood about his search for Tito. And he was still counting on Alex to include him in the search. "Call when you need help. I'm good on strategy," he'd said. As the miles fell away behind him, Alex felt oppressed by his father's silence; he missed Klema's easy ability to make talk, no matter what the situation.

Alex twisted in his sleeping bag. That damned root poked into his hip, no matter which way he turned. And now Dad was snoring, vibrating the tent's thin nylon wall. Alex got to his knees, opened the zipper slowly and carefully, and climbed out, pulling the sleeping bag after him. He took a leak, then sat under a tree huddled in his bag, watching the moonlight turn the craggy peaks to silver. He could see why so many artists had tried to paint these mountains. Perone, however, would take one look at the cliffs and want to climb them—or, worse, decide to hang glide off the top. Crazy.

For the first time, Alex wondered if Tito had hurt someone else doing one of his crazy stunts. But he didn't think that would cause his parents to kick him out.

No way to figure any of that out now. Alex slid down the tree's rough trunk, found a soft spot between two big roots, and fell into a fitful sleep.

On Friday morning, four days later, Alex sat in the living room of their little house off Rose Avenue, staring at the phone. His chest ached. Could you die of loneliness? He

touched the phone, then let go, resisting the urge to call his
sister. Dad was adamant about calling Vermont when the rates
were low, and right now was the most expensive time. Plus,
Rita would be working. She and Molly made a good team:
Molly cutting clean, straight swathes with the power mower
while Rita clipped and raked and weeded. For a minute—and
not for the first time—Alex wondered what he was doing here.

He needed to talk to Rita. Alex sighed, found a pad of
paper and a pen, and sat on the couch. This was weird. Had
he ever sent his sister a letter? Probably not. They'd always
been together, even at summer camp. He stared at the paper a
long time before he figured out what to say.

Dear Rita,

*I can't believe we've only been gone nine days—it
feels like forever. L.A. is the same, except I forgot how
endless it is when you drive in from the desert. The
house is okay; it has a patio, with a big eucalyptus tree
and a great barbecue. We cook out almost every night.
And it's close to our old neighborhood; an easy walk to
the beach.*

*Dad's at the studio, and I'm supposed to finish
unpacking, clean the place up, but I may bag that one—
I need to get out of the house. The walls are this puke
yellow color—you'll hate it. I'm going to buy an easel
pad and draw some of the animals we saw on the way
here. I hate staring at blank walls. It's weird being alone
with Dad. He doesn't say much—guess I never noticed,
with you and Mom around. When he's not at the studio,
he's at the computer here. Pretty obsessed with making
his story work. Not that I blame him.*

*Sorry. I can just see you reading this and saying to
yourself: Boy, is he depressed. But don't worry. It will
get better, as soon as I find Tito. (No word on him yet.)*

So how's hopping, stomping Griswold? How's the
lawn-mowing business? Say hi to Molly and tell
Klema I'll write soon.
    I miss you. More than I thought—

Alex signed the letter and sealed it. So much he hadn't said. He couldn't admit how lonely he was, but she'd probably figure it out anyway.

He picked up the phone and dialed a guy named Steve, who used to be on his soccer team. After Alex said his name, there was a long, awkward pause. Finally Steve said, with fake enthusiasm, "Beekman! How the hell are you? Don't tell me you're back in town."

Alex stumbled around, trying to figure out what to say next. He asked about club soccer and Steve said, "Actually, our team is filled, but call the AYSO central number and see what's up."

"Thanks. I'll do that. By the way," Alex asked casually, "any word on Tito Perone? I'm having trouble tracking him down."

"Nope. Haven't seen him in months. Try his parents, why don't you? Sorry, but I gotta go—I'm late for work." Steve said good-bye as fast as he could. Alex hung up with a red face. That was his fourth try—and his last, he decided. He called some of Rita's friends, who were more polite, but that was it. Mostly he left messages on machines and didn't expect anyone to call back.

He pulled a few books from the box that held his father's office stuff, set them on a shelf, then stared in disgust at the tracks of dust on the cheap pine. "I'm outta here," he said, surprised by how loud his voice sounded in the empty room. He went to his bedroom, dug his Rollerblades and a water bottle from a duffel bag, and put them in a backpack, along with an orange, a bagel, and his knee and wrist pads.

It was a quick walk to the beach, and as soon as he smelled the salt air and saw the hazy blue bowl of sky opening over the dark Pacific, he felt better. "This is more like it," he said out loud.

But the beach was crowded for a Friday morning. Tight packs of cyclists streamed by on the bike path, while skaters straggled along in the pedestrian lane, some of them obviously out for the first time; they clutched and grabbed each other to keep from falling. Disgusted, Alex decided to walk on the beach. He tied his shoes to his pack and picked his way through the tight family groups scattered across the sand, breathing in the smell of sunscreen and French fries. He stepped over a little girl's intricate labyrinth of moats and towers, reached the edge of the surf, and turned north.

The sand at the tide line was hard-packed. A tall guy in a skintight tank suit, his hair falling in ringlets to his shoulders, played Frisbee with himself, flipping it with a tight flick of the wrist so that it spun overhead and came back to him like a boomerang. He caught Alex's stare and winked. Alex blushed and hurried past.

No one was surfing, and as he approached Bay Street, he saw why: It was a blackball day. A small yellow flag, with a black ball in the middle, snapped from the pole near the lifeguard's station. Too many swimmers in the water, so Tito wouldn't be around. Perone wasn't keen on swimming just for the fun of it. Plus, the surf was lame.

He was about to turn back when he caught sight of a familiar profile at the lifeguard station. Alex angled up from the surf and stopped, hands on his hips. Unbelievable. Had time frozen? Hawk sat there, hunkered down as always, his nose smeared with zinc oxide, bleached blond hair streaming out from under his Angels cap—and the familiar sunglasses, the ones that seemed to reflect the whole beach, hiding his eyes. He looked blasé, but Hawk didn't miss a trick; once Alex watched him launch a boat to rescue a swimmer yanked out by a riptide before anyone else had even noticed there was a problem. That was when Alex understood the reason for Hawk's nickname.

Hawk would probably die here, Alex thought as he walked slowly toward the steps. He raised his voice to compete with the hip-hop playing inside the booth, the crackle of the two-way radio. "Hey, Hawk."

The lifeguard's head turned a fraction of an inch, then quickly straightened. "Beekman. Thought you guys had both disappeared for good."

Both? Disappointment jammed into Alex's gut.

"Where you been?" Hawk asked.

"Vermont."

Hawk's laugh was raspy, as if the sand he breathed all day had coated his throat. "Land of the inboarders. What kind of surf they got there?"

"The cold white kind. I did a little snowboarding—"

"Pitiful substitute," Hawk drawled. "Say, where's your friend Perone, anyway?"

Alex's heart sank. "I was going to ask you. You haven't seen him?"

"Naw. I thought you guys were tight."

"We kind of lost touch—we don't write letters—"

"Letters!" Hawk stood and stretched, showing the ropy muscles of his back beneath his T-shirt. His eyes never left the water. "Pick up the phone, man."

Alex didn't answer. Talking to Hawk was weird, since he only gave you half his attention—if that.

"Where's your Eberly?" Hawk asked.

"Home. The surf's no good."

"And the water's full of poison, they say—although I've never had any problems. They're talking wind change tonight, strong swells tomorrow. Come down early, we'll catch a few before my shift begins. Still a beach break here, nothing like the nice point breaks at Malibu—but we can play around, do a few lippers and aerials. You got a short board yet?"

"Nope."

"Never mind. The Eberly's a good stick."

"What time?" Alex asked, feeling psyched. Since when did Hawk, the top surfer on the beach, deign to catch waves with peasants like himself? No way he could refuse.

"Seven," Hawk said. "Or earlier." The music stopped. Without averting his eyes, Hawk reached down, turned the tape over, and punched the play button. He sank into his chair, pulled his hat low, and crossed his arms over his chest. "Take it easy," he said.

It was a dismissal, but so what? At least someone in this crazy city remembered who Alex was.

eight

B a c k   a t   t h e house, Alex felt edgy and trapped. The red light flashed on the answering machine, but both calls were for his father. He wrote the messages down, paced the living room, then strode to the phone, dialing Tito's number before he had a chance to change his mind. Mr. Perone answered, his voice froggy with a cold.

"Is Raquel there?" Alex asked quickly, praying Mr. Perone wouldn't recognize him.

"No." Tito's father coughed, and then said, "She's at work. Can I take a message?"

Alex hesitated. "Could you give me her number? I wrote it down, but I can't find it."

"Young man, The Breakers Club is in the book. Now, if you'll excuse me—" he hung up in a fit of coughing.

Alex set the phone down, grinning. That was easy. He left a note for his father, wheeled his road bike out from the patio, clipped on his helmet, and pedaled back to the beach. The bike path was still crowded, but this time he got into the challenge of it, as if he were weaving in and out of traffic on the Santa Monica Freeway. He pedaled hard into the oncoming wind, his head bent low over the handlebars. When he reached the pier, he backpedaled for a minute, remembering his dream, then zipped through quickly, holding his breath against the musty, dank smells, his eyes focused on the path.

A mile or so north, the crowds thinned. He slowed when he saw the club's green and white umbrellas, dotting the sand like flowers, jumped off his bike, and pushed it through the soft sand. He locked it to a low fence, entered the club through the beach entrance, and walked in purposefully as if he belonged there, asking for Raquel at the main desk. The tall woman behind the counter didn't even glance up from her work. "Outside, doing umbrellas and chairs."

Alex hurried away, thankful she hadn't questioned him, and stood under the striped awning a minute, scanning the little clumps of mothers, babies, and toddlers. No guys anywhere— and no Raquel. He went into the long shed, waiting in the doorway for his eyes to adjust to the dim light. At the far end of the building, a short muscular woman with dark hair, wearing the club's green shirt, wrestled with a pile of folding chairs. Alex walked quietly toward her.

"Hey, Raquel," he called softly. "Need some help?"

Tito's sister turned, squinted at him, and let out a little squeal. "Alex!" She dropped her chairs and threw her arms around his middle. "Stranger! Where did you come from?" Raquel peered up at him. Her eyes were a golden brown, lighter than Tito's, but she had her brother's infectious smile. "Were you always so tall?"

He grinned, patting her head. "Nope. Guess you shrank."

She punched his chest, about to slip into the old teasing pattern of their friendship, but then her smile evaporated. "I suppose you didn't come here just to find me."

He paused, embarrassed. "Well, I am glad to see you—but you're right, I'm looking for Tito. Where the hell is he?"

She tucked her short hair behind her ears. "It's a long story. Our parents warned Sofia and me not to talk about him."

Alex grabbed her elbows. "Raquel, he's my best friend." He took a deep breath, struggling to control his voice. "Can't you tell me anything?"

She pulled away gently and glanced at her watch. "Help me deliver these chairs—then I'll go on break, so we can talk."

· · ·

Fifteen minutes later, Alex sat with Raquel in the shade of the clubhouse, sipping lemonade. He answered her questions about his situation as quickly as he could, frustrated by the way she was avoiding the subject. Finally, he couldn't stand it anymore.

"What's going *on?*" Alex demanded.

Raquel dug her square feet into the sand. "I can't tell you."

"Why? Because you don't know? Or because you won't."

"Both. And I have no idea where he's living." She wiped her eyes with the back of her hand. "Alex, it's been horrible—"

"What did he do? Rob a bank? Murder someone?"

"No. He didn't *do* anything," Raquel said. "Except tell the truth." She gave him a long, hard look, then turned away, sifting sand over her legs.

Alex shifted uneasily, remembering his dream. "I keep having this nightmare that Tito is in trouble. Sometimes he's surfing, or sometimes he's about to fall into La Brea. I try to help him, but it's always too late." He glanced at Raquel, but she'd pulled her sun visor low over her eyes. "I know the dreams are trying to tell me something—but what?"

Raquel stayed quiet a long time. Then she said, "We don't always want to see what's right in front of us."

Alex clenched sand in his fists. "Damnit, Raquel! Everyone talks as if I have to solve some intricate Chinese riddle before I can find him."

She squeezed his knee. "Calm down. All I can tell you is that he's living in the area. He works odd jobs, but doesn't say where. I see him once in a while, and I could mention that you're around."

Alex swirled the ice in his cup. "Could you? That would be great. And I promise I won't talk to your parents. Your mother was especially scary on the phone."

Raquel sighed. "Yeah—she's really angry at Papa as well as Tito. Our father really lost it this spring." She pulled a small order pad from her hip pocket. "Give me your phone number and I'll pass it on, if he comes by."

Alex had to think a minute to remember it. As he scribbled the number down Raquel added, "I should warn you—he's changed."

"Aren't we all?"

"I guess." She brushed the sand from her legs. "Just—don't count on things being the way they were, that's all."

Alex heard the disappointment in her voice and struggled to keep the sadness from overwhelming him, too. "Is he still in school?"

"No—he dropped out this spring, but he took the GEDs." She finished her drink and stood up. "I'd better to get back to work. I'll call you if I hear anything."

"Promise?"

Her eyes filled again. She rested her head against his chest when he hugged her, then hurried away without saying good-bye.

Alex unlocked his bike and rode south, taking the Pacific Coast Highway this time. He gripped the handlebars and kept his head tucked, pedaling hard to steady himself against the passing rush of traffic. He pedaled up the steep California Incline and got off his bike, walking it along the edge of the bluffs, his eyes taking in everything: the old women in black dresses, stockings rolled around their knees, playing cards in the shade; runners jogging slowly along the dirt path next to signs reading KEEP OFF THE GRASS; people reading under the palms. A homeless man lay stretched out on one of the benches, a straw hat over his face. Alex was afraid to look closely, but the hands folded over the man's chest were too long and slender to be Tito's.

He walked all the way to the end of the park, then came

back along the Ocean Avenue side, watching everyone, but there was no sign of his friend. Besides, he couldn't imagine Tito here. This park was too laid back, a place to read and relax. Even the joggers seemed to move in slow motion.

Where the park ended he forced himself to walk out onto the pier, rolling his bike along the wooden deck. The stores had changed since he was last here, but the place still felt the same: a mix of honky-tonk, fast food, and touristy gift shops. He stopped outside the carousel, watching a few kids rise and fall on their horses like surfers on slow swells, envious of their innocence. When the breathy sound of the calliope stopped, he mounted his bike and went back to Ocean Avenue, stopping at the stationery store for an easel pad, which he balanced precariously on his handlebars all the way home.

The empty apartment was oppressive. Alex found a Muddy Waters CD and jacked the music up loud while he wiped off the shelves and unpacked his father's books. He set the empty box outside, and then sat at the kitchen table, opening the clean pad to the first page. He tried to draw an elk, then a mule deer, but he couldn't get the proportions right and ended up tearing up the pages. As he closed the pad, he found the Santa Monica newspaper his father had left on the table. He skimmed through it, surprised to find a Personals section at the back; he hadn't remembered that from the last time they lived here—or maybe he didn't care about that stuff then. At the bottom of one column, he came across this plea:

WOMAN IN BLUE, SITTING AT THE FIG TREE LAST
SUNDAY, LOST YOUR PHONE NUMBER. CRAZY FOR YOU.
CALL ME AT—

Well why not? Alex called the newspaper for information, then spent a long time composing his ad, scribbling and crossing words out:

TITO. TIME TO RIDE THOSE TUBES. WHERE ARE YOU?
BACK IN TOWN FOR THE SUMMER, LIVING IN VENICE.
CALL ME: 555–1292. NO QUESTIONS ASKED. ALEX.

He copied it over neatly and biked to the paper's Santa Monica office to catch the classified deadline. He mailed his letter to Rita, bought some stamped envelopes so he could write Molly and Klema, and went back home. Now there was nothing to do but wait—and keep looking.

nine

When Alex's alarm went off at six, he lay in bed a few minutes, huddled under his thin blanket. He wished he hadn't left the window open. His room felt clammy. And Hawk was right about the change in the weather: a stiff wind rattled the palm fronds against the stucco walls of the house. Alex fought the urge to go back to sleep and forced himself out of bed to pull on sweats over bathing trunks. He stuffed his wet suit into his backpack and went into the kitchen.

Chris Beekman stood at the table, staring out the window. He looked small and old; his shoulders slumped, his bare legs roped below the knees. His face was a pasty white, and Alex wondered if he'd even been outside since they arrived. How did a couch potato end up with a son who was a jock?

"Hey, Dad."

His father jumped, slopping his coffee. "Alex. I didn't hear you."

"Sorry. Didn't mean to spook you." Alex opened the fridge and stared at the empty shelves. "Any chance we could buy some food?"

Chris rubbed his eyes. "I was hoping you could shop later."

"Sure. But I'll need the car—"

"If you drive me to work, you can have it all day."

Alex found a bagel in the bread box, started to slice it, and then stuffed it back in the bag. He was sick of bagels. He poured himself a bowl of cereal instead. "I'm going surfing now," he said. "I'll pick up the car later, on my bike."

His father frowned. "Surfing? The rules haven't changed, even though you're older."

"Don't worry, Dad. I'm going with Hawk, the top lifeguard. If he can't save me, no one can."

Chris looked embarrassed. "Sorry. I know you're old enough to take care of yourself. Just be careful."

"Of course." Alex eyed the stack of newspapers on the counter as he ate his cereal. "Can I see the local paper?" he asked, trying to sound casual.

"Sure." Chris passed the unopened local paper over to Alex, who waited until his father was engrossed in the *L.A. Times* before looking through the Personals for his ad. Luckily, they started next to the comics, so Dad wouldn't wonder why he was fixated on that page. His ad was at the end of the last column, which was good, Alex decided; it stood out more. He ripped out the classified section and folded it up small.

His father looked up. "Find something interesting?"

"Just looking at the want ads," Alex said, flustered.

"That reminds me—the studio's weekend messenger and office boy quit, and they need to find someone fast. It's not that interesting, but some of it is outdoors. You could run errands on your bike—not a bad deal. Interested?"

"Maybe." Unfortunately, Alex had nothing better to do on weekends—or any other day, for that matter. "What should I do?"

"Call Pat Arnold. She's the office manager—a good person. When you come for the car later, I'll introduce you." Chris cleaned his glasses on his shirttail and then rattled Alex by saying, "I'm surprised you haven't seen Tito. You guys talked yet?"

Alex shook his head. "He's not around."

"That's too bad. His family away?"

"I guess. I called, but there was no answer." Alex kept his eyes averted. Right now, it was easier to lie than tell the truth.

The beach was deserted. Orange tractors idled where the sand met the pavement, ready to rake the garbage from the day before. Alex set his heavy board in the sand while he pulled on his wet suit. He had trouble zipping it. Even with his belly sucked in, the tight fabric pulled at his crotch and shoulders. Damn. He hadn't worn it for almost a year. He should have realized it would be too tight. If only he would stop growing! There was no way he could buy another one of these suits now. And being tall wasn't necessarily an asset for a surfer. The best were built short and square, like Tito—or Klema.

Alex tossed his hair off his forehead, smiling. He knew better than to complain about being too tall if Klema could hear him.

He ducked his head against the wind as he crossed the soft part of the beach. The steep troughs between the waves were dark and oily, and foam flew in mare's tails from their breaking crests. Alex gripped his board, his mouth dry with that crazy mix of fear and excitement that always hit him when he first touched the water.

He hooked on his ankle strap and waded in slowly. Even in his wet suit, the Pacific was cold. What if he'd forgotten how to do this? Someone told him once that surfing was like riding a bike: Once you learn how, you never forget. Alex knew it was more like Rita and her flute—something you needed to work at every day.

He scanned the black water out beyond the first line of breakers, where five or six guys lay on their boards, floating on the swells as if they could wait all day for the big one. But then a wave train rose majestically; two surfers saw it coming and paddled toward it. One was a small guy; a kid, Alex thought, although it was hard to tell from this distance. The small surfer tried to catch the first wave in the set, but started too late; the wave boiled over him. The second guy paddled over the first wave, then slid to his feet in a quick, fluid motion, crouching with one foot forward, his body angled up and into the wave. Alex recognized Hawk's long-legged stance. The lifeguard played with the wave on his short board, sliding into the sleek, hollow tube like a skateboarder inside a half pipe.

Alex launched himself into the surf. Hawk's wave broke over him like a bucket of loose stones. He held his breath and dove down, dragging his board behind him, then paddled hard and fast out through the remaining breakers into an area of strong swells. He floated on his board a minute to catch his breath but kept stroking steadily against the southern current, which was slowly carrying them all toward Malibu. The cold seeped through the seams of his wet suit, and his hands grew numb almost instantly, even though the air was warm. He stayed quiet a few minutes to get a feel for the surf, then paddled hard to meet a wave, catching it too late. On his third or fourth try, he finally found his balance and rode up into the wave's smooth, curving belly. His toes gripped the board as the water turned solid under his feet. For a second, he felt split in time, as if the dark water of the Pacific and the white snow of Crystal Hill, Griswold's ski area, had melded into one entity beneath him. He took two or three waves like that, exhilarated by the thrill of regaining something he thought he'd lost forever, and laughed out loud. The only thing missing was Tito.

Alex had been there for a while before Hawk paddled over. "Nice rides you're catching," he called.

"Thanks," Alex said, surprised. Hawk usually followed the surfer's code in the water: action, not talk.

"The surf's erratic," Hawk said. "And there's a riptide, farther up, near the pier—keep watch."

So Hawk was on the alert, even off duty. Alex nodded,

expecting Hawk to paddle away, but instead he pulled himself closer, his long arms slicing through the water. "Get a load of that kid," Hawk said, pointing at the smaller surfer. "The one trying to grow into his board. Tell me his Eberly doesn't look familiar."

Alex tried to see him, but a big swell rose between them. Hawk skimmed over the top and disappeared into the trough on the other side. Alex followed, keeping his eye on the kid, who couldn't be more than eleven or twelve. The boy wore a half suit, too big for his body, exposing skinny nut-brown legs. His face and arms were tan, too, as if he'd spent the entire winter out here, and his black hair was trimmed short in a punk cut. A future beach bum.

A wave started to break, then reformed, spraying foam over the kid and himself. Alex ducked his head, and when he opened his eyes, he saw the kid must have tried to ride the wave, but missed; he was paddling back out, his thin arms barely reaching into the water on each side of the board.

Alex watched the kid casually while keeping an eye on the waves that rolled steadily toward him. At first, he didn't notice anything unusual. The kid was dwarfed by his board, that was for sure; it was a beat-up Eberly like his own, with a red stripe down the middle; probably a five-eleven, much too big for the punk. But as Alex paddled closer he saw duct tape wrapped around the board's middle, and his gut turned cold. A gust of wind pushed them to the north, and the kid slid back on the board so his feet were in the water. The boy kicked hard, try-ing to keep ahead of the current, and the shift in his weight caused the board's nose to rise high, like the prow of a ship.

Alex couldn't believe what he saw. One quick glance showed him the design painted on the underside of the board: a giant sea turtle, fins outstretched like wings, her craggy head lifted toward the oncoming surf. Her underbelly's rich but-ter yellow had faded, her once dazzling copper shell was a

pale brown, but Alex would have recognized the design anywhere. He had painted one just like it under his own Eberly.

A wave broke over him, knocking him into the water. Alex
came up sputtering, reeled the Eberly back in, and scrambled
on. The boy and his board were tangled in foam; the board
jutted from the water, then spurted toward shore. The kid
swam after it; obviously he wasn't wearing a leash.

Alex started after him, then changed his mind. He'd probably come back out.

Alex paddled parallel to the beach, his heart pounding.
How the hell had this punky kid ended up with Tito's board?
Alex thought of the day he and Tito had painted the designs.
It was a hot Sunday a few weeks before they moved to
Vermont, a day too calm for surfing. They'd set everything up
at the Beekmans' because Tito's mother was a nut about
cleanliness, while Alex's parents believed messes were a sign of
creativity. Alex had worked from a photograph Tito found in a
World Wildlife publication, using paint that was supposed to
hold its color. "No matter where the sea turtle goes, she carries
her home on her back," Tito had told him.

Home. Alex tried to wrap himself around that concept, the
way his arms wrapped around his board, but it just didn't
work. Had he ever known where his home was?

A perfect roller rose before Alex. He thought of trying to
catch it, but he was too late. Instead, he pushed through, tucking his chin and kicking hard, his eyes stung by the salt. When
he came up, the kid was stripping out of his wet suit near the
lifeguard station. Alex swam to shore as fast as he could, his
board skimming over the foam, and when he reached the
beach, the kid was already struggling toward the parking lot
with his board. Alex tore off his strap, dropped the Eberly, and
chased the kid awkwardly up the beach, slowed down by the
tight wet suit.

"Hey," he called. "Wait!"

The kid turned around, surprised, and waited for Alex to catch up, watching him with pale, almost colorless gray eyes. The boy's lips were blue, and his whole body shook with cold, but he puffed out his chest as if he weren't afraid. "What do you want?" he demanded.

Alex stared him down. "You stole that board."

The kid planted the board in the sand and clutched it against his chest, looking absurdly small against it. "I didn't. It's mine," he said.

Alex grabbed his arm. "Come here. I want to show you something."

"I don't have to," the boy said. If Alex's grip hurt him, he wasn't letting it show; his chest muscles tightened but his eyes didn't flinch. "Let go of me," he complained, trying to twist away. He glanced toward the surf, where Hawk was emerging from a boiling stew of foam. "I'll tell Hawk."

Alex gave him a tight smile. "Go ahead. Hawk's the one who noticed you had Tito's board." He let the kid go, ashamed to see his finger marks on the boy's arm. "Look," Alex said, "do me a favor, and look at something with me. Leave your stick here; I won't take it."

The kid set the Eberly down. Alex leaned over, ran his fingers along the rutted fiberglass as if it might yield up some clue to his missing friend, then led the boy back to the lifeguard station. Hawk stood on the bottom step, peeling off his wet suit like a snake shedding its skin. He combed his hair back with his fingers, squinting as Alex approached. His eyes were a fierce, cold blue. Alex couldn't remember ever noticing their color before—maybe he'd never seen Hawk without his dark glasses. "You were right," he told Hawk. "It's Tito's Eberly—"

"It's mine!" the kid cried, his voice high-pitched. Alex ignored him. He picked up his own board and turned it over without saying a word. The kid stared at the sea turtle. "Hey, that's the same picture as—" he gulped, realizing he'd given himself away. Alex and Hawk stared at him, waiting. The kid's gray eyes were watery. He folded his arms over his heaving chest. "Look," he stammered, "I found it on the beach about a month ago. No one was using it. Is that a crime? It's a piece of junk. The ankle strap was broken, and it's cracked, under this tape—the guy probably didn't want it anymore."

"It's not junk. And Tito would never give up his board," Alex said. His skin crawled, as if sand fleas were running up and down inside his wet suit. He clenched his fists. He wanted to pummel the kid, but his anger had nothing to do with this measly runt who was trying to learn a big kid's sport. "Where'd you find it?" Alex demanded.

The kid pointed to a vague spot halfway to the parking lot. "It was just lying there. Above the high tide line. I came down the next day and someone had moved it to the top of the beach. It had these marks on it, like maybe the tractors hit it by mistake. So I started using it but I left it under a bench for a few days in case the guy came to get it. But he never showed up." The kid's teeth were chattering harder than ever now. "It's mine," he said again, his chin jutting out stubbornly.

Alex suddenly felt exhausted. The adrenaline rush drained from his body all at once. Maybe Tito *had* tossed his board. Was that what Raquel meant, when she said her brother had changed? "Okay," Alex said, defeated. "You can use it. But hide it here, at the top of the beach, in case Tito wants it back. What's your name?"

"Sparrow," the kid said. Alex swallowed a laugh. What a stupid name for a kid! Still, he did look like a bird, with those spindly legs. Probably his parents were old hippies, like Klema's mom. Klema claimed his mother had transformed from hippie to yuppie the day she turned forty.

Alex made Sparrow write his name and number in the notebook Hawk kept in his station, then watched him struggle toward the parking lot with the Eberly under his arm. He stowed it behind a park bench, covered it with sand, and disappeared. Alex turned to Hawk. "Strange, huh?"

Hawk nodded. "You thinking what I am?"

Alex swallowed hard. "About the broken ankle leash."

"Yeah. Perone wouldn't do something stupid, would he? Surf alone, on a bad day."

Alex didn't answer. They both knew the answer to that question.

Hawk's eyes were grave. "The sea gives up its dead eventually," he said. "Lots of ugly stuff washes up here—but no bodies. I'd be the first to know."

"That's good." Alex wished he could treat it the way Hawk did: as a casual matter. But his fingers trembled as he unzipped his suit and peeled it off. "God, I'm not used to the cold water anymore," he said, to cover himself.

Hawk poured coffee from a silver thermos and held the cup out. Alex took a sip, then handed it back. The hot liquid seared his throat. "Thanks."

"Come again," Hawk said, as if he owned the beach.

He might as well, Alex thought, watching Hawk pull on his sweats and settle into his chair, his expression hidden behind the oval mirrors of his glasses. Alex dressed and took off across the sand. His board felt waterlogged and heavy under his arm. Behind him, waves churned steadily toward the shore from distant places: Hawaii, Japan, Siberia. They would beat on the coast today, yesterday, and tomorrow, no matter what he, Alex Beekman, thought or felt about anything.

ten

Monday morning, Alex woke up with a
nasty rash all over his torso, following the outline of his wet
suit. What the hell? He checked it out in the mirror. Hawk
had warned him about the polluted water but he hadn't
taken it seriously. He considered showing the rash to his
father, but quickly ruled that one out. Dad would make the
beach off-limits forever. Instead, he covered it with zinc
oxide and a long-sleeved shirt.

A thick fog lay over the coast, muffling the sound of traffic and coating everything with clammy beads of moisture.
Alex went out back to juggle. It took him a long time to get
warm. He bounced the ball from chest to knee and from
instep to ankle, up to his head, down to his feet again, over
and over, swearing when he lost control and the ball bounced
onto the concrete. After a while, he grew tired of the uneven
rhythm and began shooting the ball against the side of the
house, dribbling a few steps, then aiming at an imaginary
goal under his bedroom window. He aimed too high twice,
smacking the glass so hard, he was sure it would break. The
third time, he scooped up the ball and carried it inside. Better
not push his luck. Besides, it was a drag playing soccer alone.

He went through the kitchen for a glass of water, turning
on lights to make the house seem less gloomy, then switching them off when he remembered his father's worries about
paying the bills. He drained his glass, ran his fingers through
his hair, and pulled on his bike helmet, suddenly anxious to
get out.

He rode up Ocean Avenue, running red lights, weaving in and out of traffic as if he were on a motorcycle, taking crazy chances. His chest felt tight and his eyes burned; he wasn't sure if it was smog, loneliness, or both.

He swung off his bike at the pier and walked it out along the deserted boardwalk. The carousel's calliope sang to riderless horses, and the bumper cars sat motionless, piled up in one corner like fish trapped in a net. Alex stopped at the end of the pier and looked down through chinks in the boards, watching the waves sluice up through the pylons. He was about to start back when he saw a shop he hadn't noticed last time he was out here, maybe because its neon lights were more luminous in the fog. A flashing green and purple sign read JIMBO'S TATTOO AND DESIGN. It was a low-slung building, skewed to one side, which looked as if it might tumble off the end during a stiff offshore wind. A grimy HELP WANTED notice was pasted at an angle on the door. The shop windows were covered with clean white paper.

Alex leaned his bike against a bench, remembering his last conversation with Tito, so many months ago, when Tito told him about piercing his ear. Hadn't he mentioned a place on the pier? Alex stepped closer to read another sign, printed in bold letters: ALL NEEDLES GUARANTEED STERILE. YOUR DESIGN OR OURS. COME IN FOR A FREE ESTIMATE.

A collage of photos filled a display case beside the door. Men and women wearing skimpy clothes posed to show off tattoos etched on their backs, arms, legs, and bellies; even their breasts and butts. The designs were intricate and featured animals, whales and dolphins, insects and butterflies, eagles and spiders. One woman had a flowering vine twisting up her leg, another had brilliant orange coral snakes tattooed around her arms. Alex shuddered, and was about to turn away when something caught his eye: a turtle painted on a shoulder blade. A long, black ponytail dangled next to the design. Alex bounced nervously on his toes. What the hell was *his* turtle design doing in the window of a tattoo shop? No doubt about it: This sea turtle matched the ones swimming across the undersides of his and Tito's boards.

Alex stared at the picture for a long time. It couldn't be Tito's back: He didn't have such long hair. But Perone must have been here—or, at least, given the design to someone else who decided to use it as a tattoo. Better go in and check the place out. Alex locked his bike to the bench, took a deep breath, and pushed the door open.

He expected a sleazy shop, but he entered a clean, well-lit room, which smelled like a cross between a hospital lab and a paint store. Tattoo designs covered every inch of wall space, like a cluttered art gallery. In the center of the room was a tall, padded table, surrounded by folding parchment screens. Banks of instruments filled a counter stretched across the back wall. In the far corner, three full-length mirrors made a small cubicle, like a dressing room in a fancy department store.

A man stepped out from behind the screen, pulling on a shirt. "Howdy," he said. "Another victim?" Before Alex could answer, the man pointed to his chest. "Take a look at Jimbo's latest creation."

Alex felt the way he did in a reptile house at the zoo: half repelled, half fascinated. He edged closer. The man turned on a crookneck lamp resting on a small table and swiveled, aiming the light at his shaved chest. The tattoo showed the sun setting over the sea while the moon rose from behind the mountains—an image Alex had carried in his own mind after they'd left L.A. "Nice, huh?" the man said, looking up at him. "Designed it myself. Takes Jimbo to transform it into art, though."

Alex swallowed hard, wondering how many needle jabs it took to create such a big picture. "Yeah, it looks great." He cleared his throat, looking around. "So, is Jimbo the owner?"

"One and the same." A swarthy bald man with a thick, curling beard appeared from the back, drying his hands on a towel. "I'm Jimbo."

Alex couldn't help staring. The man's shorts and sleeveless denim shirt revealed plenty of skin—every inch of it covered with tattoos of different colors. The colored images rippled and changed as he moved. A Bengal tiger peered out from inside his shirt, which was open almost to his navel. Intricate tribal designs—black hooks interwoven with barbed arrows—danced up and down his arms. Only his hands and face were clear. Alex wondered about the parts of his body he couldn't see, and hoped the guy wouldn't turn around; no telling what he'd see on the back of that shaved head. The man's liquid brown eyes skimmed over Alex, as if he were picturing where to set the needles for his next design. "Here for a tattoo?"

"Well—not exactly. I wanted to ask about the turtle design outside."

"Turtle?" Jimbo's thick eyebrows furrowed. "Oh, right. The amber sea turtle. Take a look around while I finish with my customer; then we'll talk."

Alex wandered around the room, studying the designs on the walls. He stopped in front of a row of animals, clumsily drawn. He could do better, but of course he wouldn't say so—maybe they were Jimbo's.

Jimbo talked to the client about how to care for his new tattoo. "Keep it clean and dry," Jimbo said. "No sunbathing or swimming until it's healed—you'll wreck the color. It will itch like hell, but that's normal. Any swelling, give me a call."

Alex picked up a magazine called *Skin and Ink*. He leafed through, astonished by the designs, which people wore like bodysuits. Not for me, he thought, and closed the magazine.

As Jimbo followed his client to the door, Alex saw that Jimbo did, indeed, have a tattoo on the back of his shaved scalp: A lightning bolt streaked from a cloud onto his neck.

He grinned. Wait until Klema heard about this.

"Now, let's take a look at that turtle," Jimbo said.

Alex followed him outside. The sun was burning through the fog, turning the air a sickly gray yellow. Alex pointed to the photograph in the display case.

"Right," Jimbo said. "That was a tricky one. An original design—the guy brought it in himself. We had fun with it— when he flexes his muscle, the turtle seems to swim."

Alex bounced on his toes, trying to contain his excitement. That sounded like a typical Perone move. "It wasn't a guy named Tito Perone, was it? He mentioned getting his ear pierced here."

Jimbo suddenly seemed interested in the view of the Pacific. He kept his face turned away. "So many people pass through here every day, and I'm not so good on names. Why do you ask?"

Was Jimbo hedging? "I recognized the turtle," Alex explained. "It's just like one I painted on my surfboard a couple of years ago. I put it on my friend Tito's board, too."

Jimbo turned to face him, his dark eyes intense. "That's your drawing? I'm impressed. So you're an artist."

Alex hesitated, pleased. He'd never thought of himself that way. "Maybe someday. I draw for fun. Mostly animals, birds, landscapes—I'm not so good at people." As Alex stared at the turtle, he had a sudden inspiration. He pointed to the HELP WANTED sign. "Are you looking for someone to work on new designs?"

Jimbo rubbed his hand over his smooth head. "I hadn't thought about it that way exactly—but it's an interesting idea. Come back inside." He put up a CLOSED sign as they went in. When Jimbo bent over a small fridge to pull out two sodas, Alex had a full view of a monarch butterfly flying up his right thigh.

"Care for a Coke?" Jimbo asked.

"Fine." Alex took the soda and popped open the top, glad to

have something to do with his hands. "What's the job like?" he asked.

"I need someone to help in the late afternoons and early evenings. You'd clean up after me, help people pick a design, maybe hand out brochures on a slow day to lure people in—that kind of thing." Jimbo drained his soda. "I'd like to see your drawings. Kids often pick animals, especially the ones getting their first tattoos. If you're interested, you could bring in some animal sketches, give me a sense of your style. What did you say your name was, anyway?"

"Alex. Alex Beekman." Alex sat forward in his chair to shake Jimbo's hand. In spite of his qualms about needles, this place was beginning to sound interesting. Working here would sure beat hanging out alone all day. And maybe he could track Tito down. He set his Coke on the table. "There's just one thing—I don't like needles much."

Jimbo's beard made it hard to see whether he was smiling or frowning, but his tone of voice was friendly enough. "No problem. The actual tattooing is my job. 'Course, a handsome guy like you would be a great advertisement if you had a nice little tattoo on your arm or leg. With your pale coloring, we'd get a good contrast."

"No thanks," Alex said quickly.

Jimbo set his soda can in a box of empties on the fridge. "You won't get AIDS here, if that's what you're worried about. I run a clean shop, and the needles are sterile. Let me show you around; then you can decide if it's something you want to try."

He took Alex to the back of the room and pointed to a poster of a swarthy dark man, his body tattooed from head to foot. "Tattooing is an ancient art," Jimbo said. "The word comes from Tahiti or Samoa—this young warrior is Samoan. Handsome devil, isn't he?" Alex swallowed hard, captivated by the strange beauty of this naked man whose clothing was etched onto his skin. The man in the picture stood with his legs apart, his gaze bold yet inviting.

Alex felt his palms turn clammy. He was relieved when Jimbo led him to a counter beside the curtained booth where his tools were laid out in neat rows. "This is the needle bar," Jimbo said, holding up an instrument like a dentist's drill. "It's a little like a sewing machine—the same up and down action." Alex reached out, but Jimbo blocked his hand. "Don't touch—we wear latex gloves around the equipment—a new pair for each client. Don't want anyone going home with hep B. I clean every surface with bleach—that will be your job, if I'm busy—and I'll show you how to use the autoclave." He pointed to a small silver oven. "That's where I sterilize everything. Razor blades, needles—"

"What are the razors for?"

"We shave off the hair before we tattoo—even if it's just peach fuzz."

"I didn't realize it was so complicated," Alex said.

"It's an art form. At least, that's how I see it. Look, here's my ink palette—just like any artist's." He held out a small paper plate, which held a dozen tiny red caps, each filled with bright ink, in colors progressing from light to dark. Alex longed to take a tiny brush and make a painting with the brilliant inks, but he kept still and listened as Jimbo explained how he transferred a design from a stencil onto the waiting client's skin.

"So," Jimbo said when he was done. "What do you think? Try it out for a few days?"

"All right," Alex said. And then, because he knew he might have trouble with his father over this one, he added, "I'll have to talk to my dad—"

"No problem. If he's worried, tell him to come in for the tour, or give me a call." Jimbo gave Alex his business card, then checked his watch. "Let's give each other a trial period—

say, a few days. Tomorrow looks slow, which would give you a chance to walk through things. Why don't you come in around three, and we'll see how we work together. Sound okay?"

"Fine." Alex was pleased. This was the first time that he'd found a job on his own, without his parents bugging him with a string of suggestions. He gave Jimbo his address and phone number and then, as he was about to leave, he asked, "About that sea turtle—"

Jimbo looked puzzled. "I thought you were afraid of needles."

"I am. I just wondered—if there's some way you could remember who got the tattoo."

Jimbo picked up some scraps of paper and stuffed them in the trash can. "That's confidential. I keep records, of course, because when clients want to remove a tattoo, they need to know the exact name and color of the pigment, but I don't release the information." His smile was only polite this time. "If you're interested in using that design yourself, it's easy to transfer it from the picture in the window onto a stencil."

"Thanks. Maybe some other time." Better drop it, Alex decided. Jimbo was like Hawk—a guy who didn't like to be pushed.

"See you tomorrow," Jimbo said, and disappeared behind the screen.

Alex went outside and stood at the end of the pier, leaning against the railing. The Pacific lived up to its name today; the swells were calm and the waves hissed gently across the sand. Something funny was going on here. Jimbo was avoiding his questions, which made Alex think the guy knew something about Tito. He felt both nervous and excited. Jimbo seemed pretty decent. Maybe he'd ease up on the secrecy stuff once they got to know each other better. If not . . . well, there might be other ways to get the information. Alex drummed the rail-

ing with his fingers. Patience wasn't one of his better qualities.
But he could learn—

Right. Try again, Beekman.

Alex turned to study the turtle one last time. It was certainly his design. No doubt about that. And who else in this
town had access to that sea turtle but Tito Perone? There was
that kid, Sparrow—but he didn't have a tattoo. Alex had seen
him without a wet suit and he didn't have a tattoo on his
shoulder. He wasn't the type. Alex grinned. He finally had
some information for Klema, and something to hold on to
himself—even if it was as elusive as a sea creature swimming
across a piece of paper.

eleven

Before his father came home, Alex wrote a letter to Klema, telling him everything he'd learned. He took it to the mailbox on Rose Avenue, then went back to the house and sketched as many animals as he knew how to draw, concentrating on the creatures who'd jumped out at them crossing the Rockies: elk, mule deer, rabbits, coyote. He also drew some birds, including a golden eagle, which he and his father had seen circling a parking lot in a dusty New Mexico town. He wasn't satisfied with any of them, but Jimbo had definitely said sketches, so he decided it wasn't a big deal.

Then he marinated chicken breasts in a mix he'd learned from Molly: tamari, mustard, lemon juice, and wine. He made a salad, cooked some rice, and lit the gas barbecue. The chicken was grilling by the time Chris drove in, the sweet smoky fumes drifting across the patio and into the kitchen.

"Smells good," Chris said, leaning through the back door. His brown eyes sparkled a bit behind his glasses. "What's the occasion?"

"I got a job," Alex said, "with more hours than they offered at the studio."

"Great!" Chris clapped him on the shoulder. "Let me wash up—then you can tell me all about it."

Alex turned the chicken and ladled sauce over the top. How could he make Jimbo's shop sound good?

Chris came out in a few minutes, wearing shorts and a T-shirt that barely covered his potbelly, carrying a soda and a bowl of chips. "So where are you working?"

Alex hesitated, then plunged in. "A tattoo shop on the pier." When his father's jaw jutted forward, Alex held up his hand. "Hold on, Dad. It's not what you think. The place is clean, and the guy who runs it is really careful. He wears gloves, and sterilizes everything. And he's like an artist. He really cares about doing a good job."

"But Alex, *needles?* In this day and age?"

"Dad, you know how I feel about that. Remember how I used to scream when I had my shots? Anyway, the tattooing is Jimbo's job. I'm just the handyman. I'll keep things clean," Alex said, careful to omit the fact that he might end up sterilizing the needles. "I'll pass out leaflets, help people choose their designs." His father was still frowning. "Listen, Dad. He's interested in my drawings. He might let me create some tattoo designs—"

"Of all the ways to display your work! Do you get to sign your name? You'd have one-man shows walking around town."

Alex laughed, relieved that his father was softening. "It's weird—but hey, who cares? Jimbo said you could come and meet him, if you're worried about me working there." Alex had a sudden flash of inspiration. "You know, Dad, you should write about Jimbo. He's a real character, with tattoos all over his body. He says the movie stars are getting them now—it's big fashion. He knows the history of tattooing, how Captain Cook learned the word *ta-tu* from people in the South Pacific—you could put him in a screenplay."

Chris munched on a chip, his small brown eyes flickering with interest. Alex smiled to himself. He'd caught him.

"All right, all right," his father said. "The story idea is a good one. But no tattoos for you, okay? I can't stand the thought of anyone mutilating your smooth, perfect skin." He took off his glasses, a sure sign he was embarrassed. "That makes it sound as if you're still a little kid—I know you're not, but I guess a parent always feels a kind of ownership over his child's body—which is ridiculous. Especially since someday, your body will belong to your wife—"

Alex busied himself with the barbecue. This conversation was getting out of hand. As far as he was concerned, his body didn't belong to anyone but himself right now—which was fine with him. He bit his lip to keep from saying anything else. More than anything, he really wanted that job.

"Have you thought about the risk of AIDS?" his father asked.

"Relax, Dad." Alex poured the last of the barbecue sauce over the chicken, watching it flare up, then sizzle onto the coals. "I'm not planning to cover myself with snakes and devils." But even as Alex made the promise, he was silently wondering if he could get over his fear of needles. He had a vivid image of a sea turtle, fins spread wide, neck extended, gliding smoothly and gracefully across his shoulder blade, a turtle swimming in search of its lost partner.

When Alex arrived at the tattoo shop the next afternoon, the screens were set up around the booth, and a small engine hummed.

"Who's there?" Jimbo called.

"It's me, Alex."

"Come in. She's decent."

Alex slipped behind the screens. A thin young woman, wearing shorts and a tank top, lay face down on the table. Jimbo gave Alex a curt nod and kept on working. Alex took a deep breath and forced himself to watch, hoping he wouldn't blow it by feeling queasy. The needle jabbed into the woman's arm, tracking up and down like a sewing machine. Ink oozed out from under the needle. Jimbo swabbed as he worked, keeping the skin clean. In spite of having such big hands, his work was quick and precise.

"Don't move, Shelly," Jimbo warned. "Meet Alex, my new helper."

"Hi." Shelly gave Alex a wan smile through her hair, which had fallen across her cheek. A tear trickled down her nose. "Hurts like hell," she said.

"It's painful," Jimbo said, "but you live through it."

"I hope." Shelly winced and asked Alex, "You getting a tattoo?"

"Maybe."

Jimbo raised a dark eyebrow. He kept a steady pressure on the foot pedal as he worked. "I'm giving Shelly a rose. Now she'll always have flowers, even when her girlfriend forgets her birthday."

Shelly licked the tears from the corner of her mouth. "What makes you think I have a *girl*friend?" she asked, her voice saucy in spite of her discomfort.

"Just guessing, from something you said earlier." Jimbo wiped Shelly's face with a clean tissue, then changed to a different needle. The next line came out pink as he started to draw the petals. "None of my business, really, talking about your love life."

"That's okay," Shelly said. "Maybe someday I'll be ready to put my initials and hers on the other arm."

"She going to like this rose?" Jimbo asked.

"She better. All this pain ought to be worth *something*— OW!"

Alex stared as the rose grew and blossomed on the woman's upper arm. The conversation blew him away. Imagine what Tovitch would say if he'd heard this woman talk about her lesbian lover: He'd be pulling out every half-baked insult in the book. But Jimbo acted as if he could care less who Shelly took to bed.

The bell on the door jangled. Jimbo lifted his foot, stopping the motor, and glanced at Alex. "See who's there, will you?"

Alex stepped from behind the screen and greeted a burly man. "Can we help you?" Alex asked.

"Like to put a tattoo on my arm," the man said.

"Know what you want?"

"Not really."

Jimbo came out and introduced himself without shaking hands; his rubber gloves were still taped tight around his wrists. "I'm working on a client. Alex here will show you the designs. Pick something you like and then we'll schedule an appointment. A three-inch tattoo, like the one I'm doing here, takes about an hour."

The burly man leaned into the booth, took a quick look at Shelly's shoulder, and shook his head. "Easier to have it done to you than to watch someone else get stuck."

Alex took the man around the room and waited while he picked out an intricate design of a fallen angel, which Jimbo said he'd have to do in one long session or two short ones; Alex helped him make the appointment. "Does it hurt?" the guy called out as he was leaving.

Jimbo's deep chuckle sounded from behind the screens. "The most common question in my shop. Sure it does. Still, eighty percent of my customers come back for more. Maybe they're all masochists—but they're still alive."

For the next few hours, Alex learned on the run. Jimbo gave him terse instructions, and Alex tried to fill in the gaps. He greeted other potential customers and soon learned that many hadn't worked up their nerve to get a tattoo; they just wanted to study the possible designs and then think about it. Jimbo taught him the rules: when to wear gloves, when to take them off, what he could touch with bare hands. He showed him how to wipe down all the exposed surfaces with a bleach and water solution, how to break the heads of the used needles and dispose of them in a special dispenser. He had Alex stand close while he sterilized the new needles in the autoclave. "After you've watched a few times, you can try it on your own," he said.

When they had a quiet moment, Alex unfolded a big piece of easel paper and showed Jimbo his sketches. Jimbo studied them carefully, then circled an osprey, a panther lounging on a tree branch, and an elk with a full rack of antlers, standing on a small knoll, its head held high. "These are the best," he said. "See if you can develop them a little more, add some detail—and we'll put them up on the wall."

Alex couldn't hide his smile. He folded the paper and put it in his backpack, glad to have a reason to keep drawing. This, at least, should impress his father.

Jimbo made some notes on Shelly's card and stuck it into a pink file folder. He was about to put it in the filing cabinet on the back wall when the door jangled again. A stocky man with more tattoos than Jimbo threw the door open, and Jimbo burst out laughing.

"Rich! Don't tell me *you're* back. There's no space left on your body, man!"

His friend shook his head. "Wrong. Lots of room on the edge of my back. I want one of those fallen angels we talked about."

Jimbo nodded. "Everyone's into Lucifer these days. What's the deal?"

Rich looked disappointed. "Damn. I thought it was such an original idea. And I brought my own design," he said.

"Good. Let's have a look." Jimbo handed Alex Shelly's file. "Stick that in the right place, will you? We're sexist here—pink for the ladies, in the top drawer, blue for the guys."

Alex went to the filing cabinet behind the screens while Jimbo talked to his friend. The files were in alphabetical order. Shelly's last name was McClaren, which confused him until he found McCormick. He was about to come around the screens when he realized Jimbo and Rich were still talking—and they couldn't see him. Quickly, before he lost his nerve, he bent to the lower drawer, slid it open, and flipped the files forward until he came to the *P* section. Paxton, Peltier—there it was. Perone. His fingers trembled. He cocked his head; Jimbo was still talking. He picked up the file, his eyes devouring what little information Jimbo had scrawled there. Under "Address," Jimbo had drawn a straight line. But there was a phone number. 310-555–6336. Alex glanced at Jimbo's notes below; they seemed to be names of dyes and pigments. At the bottom of the card, he had scrawled *Sea turtle, left shoulder blade, 4.* And the date: *June 1.*

A month ago. Alex found a pen on top of the file, copied the phone number on the inside of his wrist with a shaking hand, and shoved the file back in the drawer, closing it as quietly as he could.

"Alex, what's keeping you?" Jimbo called.

"Sorry—I got confused about where to file McClaren." Alex hurried around the screens. "I remember a librarian explaining where Mc comes in the alphabet, but I forgot." He smiled, hoping he didn't look too guilty. His T-shirt was glued to his back with sweat, even though the shop was cool inside. Jimbo didn't seem to notice. Another customer was on her way in.

The next hours dragged. As Alex swept the pavement outside the shop, filled the needle tube with ink, changed the display of photos in the window, the numerals on his wrist seemed to vibrate. Tito's number. He actually had his number. Unbelievable.

At five, Jimbo finished with a big, ruddy-faced woman and ushered in a tall guy, a few years older than Alex. He had what Alex and Tito used to call the "L.A. look"—someone obsessed with his body. His skin was bronzed, and his chest, when he unbuttoned his shirt, revealed pecs that made Alex jealous. The guy probably *lived* in some weight room. He couldn't help stealing glances in his direction, but when Jimbo pressed his foot on the pedal to start cutting, Alex looked away. Now he understood what his father meant about needles slashing unblemished skin.

Jimbo noticed. "Those needles still getting to you?" he asked.

"A little." Alex busied himself tidying the waiting area. God, if the job was going to mess him up this way, maybe it wouldn't work.

"I could use some help here," Jimbo called.

Alex went back reluctantly, pulled on a pair of gloves, and handed Jimbo the instruments he needed. He couldn't keep his eyes off the customer's smooth skin, slowly rippling with yellow and black as Jimbo etched a butterfly onto his shoulder.

When the client—whose name was Jason—was done, he went to the three-way mirror. He called Alex over while Jimbo cleaned up, craning his neck to see the monarch. "What do you think—should I put something on the other side? Make it more symmetrical?"

"Whatever," Alex mumbled.

"You like your job here?" Jason asked.

"It's my first day," Alex said.

Jason smiled. His eyes were an intense blue. "Could have fooled me. You seem like a pro." He handed Alex his shirt. "Help me get it on, will you? I have to admit, it hurts more than I expected."

Alex held up the shirt and guided Jason's arms into the sleeves. He was relieved when the door closed behind him.

Jimbo checked his watch. "You're done for today. And you learn quickly. The work feel all right to you?"

"It's weird," Alex admitted, "but I like it."

"Good. I'll see you tomorrow then, same time, and maybe you can stay longer, if we're busy. I'll start you at six-fifty an hour. If things work out, I'll raise you in a few weeks. I'll give you credit, on the wall, for your original designs. And you get a discount on all tattoos—if you change your mind about the needles. Sound fair?"

"Yeah, that's great," Alex said. "I'm actually thinking about a tattoo, but my dad had a fit about the job—I'll need to break him in gently."

Jimbo laughed. "Sounds like a smart plan."

As Alex was unlocking his bike, he felt a hand on his shoulder. He whirled around. Jason stood behind him, grinning. "Easy, guy." He twirled a set of keys from a long chain. "Like to grab a coffee somewhere?"

Alex felt as if he'd swallowed a handful of steel wool. His voice came out muffled and scratchy. "Uh—no thanks."

Jason regarded him with a half smile, his blue eyes dazzling in the slanting light. "Funny—I could have sworn you showed an interest. But hey, that's cool. Maybe some other time."

Alex fumbled with his bike lock and dropped the key on the planking. Jason scooped it up before Alex could get it, his fingers lingering when he pressed the key into Alex's palm. The hair on Alex's arms prickled with alarm. "You're younger than I thought," Jason said. "You seeing anyone here?"

The sharp edge of the key dug into his fingers. Alex hesitated for a split second. Would it be a crime to have coffee with the guy? He was just being friendly. But then Jason winked and a warning bell went off inside Alex's head. He spun his bike around. "Listen," he said, "I don't know what you want—but I have to go home."

Jason shrugged. "No problem. I'm in the West L.A. book, if you change your mind. Jason Kirkpatrick." He turned and sauntered out the boardwalk toward the restaurant perched at the end.

Alex swung onto his bike, his heart pounding before he even started pedaling. He rode like a maniac, nearly colliding with two old women, and just missing a dog asleep in the sun. He felt as if Tovitch's label had followed him here, just as Rita had predicted.

But he couldn't blame this on Tovitch. Randy was three thousand miles away. So what made Jason, a guy out cruising for a date, pick on Alex?

Even the strong wind rushing over him couldn't cool his burning face. Alex was halfway home before he remembered the phone number scrawled on the inside of his wrist.

He swerved onto the sidewalk on Ocean Avenue and pulled up by a pay phone. He took eight or ten long, deep breaths before he dialed, then plugged one ear against the rush of traffic. The phone rang eight times. He was about to hang up when a man's sleepy voice mumbled, " 'Lo?"

"Hello," Alex said. "Is—is Tito Perone there?"

The silence was so long that Alex said, "Hello?" again, certain they'd been disconnected.

"Who's calling?" the voice finally asked.

"Alex. Alex Beekman."

This time he heard a click, as if he'd been switched to another line. After a while, the man returned and said, "I'm sorry. There's no one here by that name."

"Wait—" But the line was dead. Alex slammed the receiver against the wall of the booth, then rode away, leaving it dangling. He was sure of two things: Tito was there. And for some reason, he didn't want to talk to Alex. Who was once his best friend.

Once, Alex thought, blinking hard to keep back the tears. Once his best friend. No more.

At home, Alex answered his father's questions about the new job in monosyllables and was relieved when Chris pushed his chair back angrily at the end of dinner. "Since you have so little to say, I guess I'll get back to work and leave you with the dishes."

Alex stared at his father's retreating back. "Thanks for *asking* me to wash up," he said under his breath. He waited until Chris was settled at the computer, his headset firmly in place, before taking the portable phone and the heavy L.A. directory into his room.

He called the information operator and asked if she could tell him the name and address of the person who had Tito's number.

"I'm sorry, sir," she said. "We're not allowed to give out that information."

"Please—it's important!" Alex begged. His mind groped for an idea. "I met this beautiful—girl," he said, stammering. "I want to send her flowers. All I know is her first name—and her phone number. If I call her, I'll spoil the surprise."

The operator was quiet a minute. "Let me connect you with my supervisor," she said at last.

This time, Alex was ready with a more embellished story. "It's in the name of love," he pleaded with the supervisor, using his softest, deepest voice, and she gave in. "All right," she said. "But don't tell anyone." The phone was listed under Ken Stein, at 3121 Weasel Creek Road.

Alex thanked her profusely. "I should send *you* flowers."

"You do that, hon. It's been a long time."

Alex returned the phone to the living room, picked up his father's map book, and found the street in the index. His heart raced. Weasel Creek Road was in Topanga Canyon, a narrow, twisting ribbon full of switchbacks.

He closed the spiral book and stood beside his father, waiting until he noticed him. Chris pulled off his headphones. He was listening to a wishy-washy show tune. Alex couldn't believe his father's taste in music.

"What is it?" Chris asked, obviously annoyed.

"Sorry, Dad. I just wondered if I could have the car tomorrow. I'll drive you to work."

"Sure. We'll figure out the details in the morning." He glanced at his watch. "I have to rewrite this scene tonight."

"No problem." Alex leaned against the door frame, watching his father disappear into his other world. He suddenly remembered all the nights when he and Rita were younger. No matter where they lived, Dad would be typing away someplace, first on a typewriter then, later, on a computer, always shut off from them by his headset. Alex and Rita would hang out with their mother, kicking the soccer ball around, reading stories, cooking together. When Alex and Rita were older, they wanted to be with their friends and their mother was left alone. He suddenly felt anxious. Maybe his parents didn't mind leading separate lives. Would Dad ever go back to Vermont? Alex felt torn. Part of him hoped he would stay, that the show would be a success—so Alex could stick around. Part of him missed his sister and mother, and Molly. Klema, too. He went to his room. First things first. Tomorrow, he'd find Tito. After that, he could decide what to do with the rest of his life.

Alex flopped on the bed, laughing. Sure. Who was he kidding?

He reached under the bed, pulled out his easel pad, and began to draw again. Tattoo ideas flowed from his fingers: wandering vines, turtles, devils, eagles, and his first attempt at a human figure in years: a surfer skimming down the side of a triple overhead, his arms outstretched, his body arced away from his feet at an impossible angle. The surfer was short and stocky, with black, almond-shaped eyes.

"Watch out, Perone," Alex said softly. "I'm coming to get you."

He jumped up, grabbed a CD and, in defiance of his father's music, played the Red Hot Chili Peppers at top volume, dancing alone between the twin beds until sweat poured down his face and his body ached with exhaustion.

twelve

Alex drove into Topanga Canyon slowly, but somehow missed Weasel Creek Road. He stopped to check the map book, saw he'd gone too far, and took the switchbacks even more carefully going down. Parts of Topanga were still fairly wild, although there were more fancy houses than he remembered, some perched on stilts or hugging the sides of steep hills. First to go in The Big One, Alex thought.

"Damn!" He braked suddenly for a dog that trotted from the woods.

No, not a dog, a coyote; a beautiful, blue-gray creature. Alex pulled over onto the shoulder to watch. The coyote was small and lithe, its movements fluid and purposeful. It seemed oblivious to the cars swerving and squealing to avoid it. One minute, it was trotting easily along the pavement, its head held high, its tail parallel to the ground—and the next instant, it melted into the chaparral.

Damn! Alex banged the dashboard in admiration. Imagine if he could pull a disappearing act like that one! Especially when Tovitch was around. He jumped out of the car and peered up the hill, hoping he might see it again. The scrub oaks and sumac pulsed with heat, but nothing moved in the underbrush.

He drove in a slow line of cars, snaking down the canyon. The Weasel Creek Road sign was small and faded, tacked to a live oak tree. No wonder he hadn't seen it.

The road quickly became dirt, and for a minute, if it hadn't been for the hot, dry air shimmering in the chaparral and the silvery green of the eucalyptus trees, he might have imagined he was back in Vermont. Talk about "old hippies"; Klema wouldn't believe these houses. He passed a tepee, a yurt with Tibetan prayer flags snapping in the wind, and houses with crazy additions. Many had solar collectors or windmills.

He stopped near a house where chickens scratched in the dusty yard and read the number on the mailbox: 2319. He was crawling now, his heart hammering as he drew up beside number 3121, trying to see around the curve in the driveway. What was he doing? Should he just forget the whole thing, while he still had a chance? After all, Tito had made it damn clear he wanted nothing to do with him.

"Come on." Alex tried to psyche himself up. "You can't quit now. He might not even be home."

He bounced along a narrow track through the chaparral, his surfboard lurching from side to side in the back of the station wagon. He rounded a sharp corner and nearly collided with an ancient gray passenger bus parked in the shade of two eucalyptus trees. A stovepipe poked from the rear of the bus, and maroon curtains covered some of the windows.

Alex shut off the engine, but clutched the steering wheel to keep his hands steady. Although there was no sign of life anywhere, a picnic table held the debris of a meal—two Pizza Hut boxes and an empty soda bottle—and laundry swung on a line that stretched from the end of the bus to a eucalyptus branch. Alex climbed out and did a double take when he took a closer look at the clothesline. A purple shirt with a Natural Progression Surfboards logo flapped in the wind. That was the shop where he and Tito used to drool over the boards they could never buy: sweet narrow guns, long triple fins. They'd go from there to Casa Mia restaurant, across the street, and console themselves with sopapillas drenched in honey. And he remembered when Tito had saved enough money to buy himself that shirt.

So. He was here.

Alex took a deep breath to steady himself and climbed the steps. A curtain was pulled across the bus door. He knocked and waited. Silence. He banged harder, and this time heard a groan. "Who is it?" someone called. After his experience on the phone with these guys, Alex didn't dare answer. Instead, he knocked again. Finally, the curtain drew back and the door opened.

A stranger stood in front of him. A stranger with long, ebony hair falling to bare shoulders, a hoop earring in one ear, and a fresh, ugly scar crisscrossing one cheek. Only the eyes were familiar. They were older, full of caution, and something Alex couldn't name—but they were Tito's.

They stared at each other a long moment. "Hey, Perone," Alex said at last. His insides churned and tumbled as if he'd caught the lip of a wave on his board and been upended by the surf. He wanted to grab Tito and hold on, but his friend's distant expression made his gut run cold.

"So you found me," Tito said finally in a low, flat voice. "Let me get some clothes on—I don't want to wake Ken." He pointed to the picnic table. "Have a seat—I'll be right out."

As he turned around, Alex saw the turtle swimming across Tito's left shoulder blade. The tattoo was bigger than he'd imagined, about the size of a sand dollar, inked in the same bronze and yellow colors as the sea turtle on the Eberly.

Alex was too restless to sit. A hot, dry wind tugged the laundry line back and forth and rattled the chaparral like old bones. A Santa Ana, as his father had predicted this morning.

The soda bottle blew off the table onto the hard-packed ground. As Alex stooped to pick it up, he discovered Tito's old Adidas ball, his favorite number six, under the bench. He pulled it out. The ball was soft. He tried to juggle, but without air, the ball careened drunkenly from one leg to the other. Alex squeezed it between his hands, kneading it like bread, then let it drop to the ground as his friend came out of the bus.

Alex bit his lip. Tito took the steps one at a time, like an old man. Although his body looked lean and hard, he limped across the dirt yard, dragging one leg. As he came closer, Alex noticed another scar, this one long and straight, below the knee. Tito had pulled his hair back, which only accentuated the raw red line running from jaw to cheekbone. He set a bottle of juice on the table between them and eased himself onto the bench across from Alex, his hurt leg stretched out at an angle.

"Jesus," Alex whispered. "What happened to you?"

"It's a long story." Tito eased opened the bottle and took a sip, then passed it to Alex. "You should have seen me three months ago. I was in a cast from hip to ankle. I'm doing better now—got the cast off a few weeks ago, and I'm starting to walk without crutches. The physical therapist says I'll be back to normal by the end of the summer, but I have my doubts. I've got a pin here"—he pointed to the scar—"I broke my tibia pretty badly."

"Damn." Alex's head was spinning. If he was lucky, this weird encounter would turn out to be a dream. "You have a car accident?"

"Nothing that simple." Tito took another long swig from the bottle of juice. "Sorry I haven't been in touch. I saw your ad in the paper—it gave me a jolt. And then Raquel told me she'd seen you. I was tempted to call—but I was afraid you'd give me away to my parents."

Alex was stung. "Gee, thanks. Glad to hear how much you trust me."

"Listen, I can't take any chances."

"Perone—I thought we were friends. Hell, you're my *best* friend. Aren't you?" Alex's voice broke. Tito didn't answer his question, and Alex nervously drummed the table with the tips of his fingers.

"How'd you find me?" Tito asked at last.

"Through Jimbo, at the tattoo shop. I saw the turtle design in his display window and realized you must have been in there."

Tito's dark eyebrows drew together. "Dammit! Jimbo promised he'd keep his mouth shut—"

"Don't worry, he did." Alex was getting royally pissed now. "I'm working there. I found your name in the file when he wasn't looking." Alex stood up. "Sounds like you wish I hadn't." Tito's silence only made Alex feel worse. "Listen, Perone. I don't give a shit what you did, even if you committed some weird crime. And I would never give you away. You should know that by now."

Tito rested his chin in his hand so his fingers covered his scarred cheek. "A crime? That's funny. You'd think I was a mass murderer, if you listened to my parents. As far as I'm concerned, I haven't done anything wrong. Except to tell the truth." He gave Alex a sad smile. "Frankly, Beekman, I'm surprised you haven't figured it out by now."

Alex drew his leg back and sent the limp soccer ball spiraling across the yard. He gripped the table, leaning close to Tito. "Why does everyone say that! It's Rita who's got ESP, not me! You have to spell it out—"

"Cool it, Beekman." Tito turned his head and his face lit up. "Hey, Ken." Alex followed his gaze. A tall, thin guy with rumpled sandy hair stood in the doorway of the bus. He reminded Alex of someone, but he couldn't think who.

"Ken, come meet Alex." Tito motioned him over. Ken stumbled sleepily down the steps, rubbing his bare chest. They shook hands, and Alex felt uncomfortable; Ken's hazel eyes were definitely sizing him up behind his wire-rimmed glasses. Tito watched them, a smile playing across his face.

"Funny I never noticed," he said. "You guys really look alike, except for the eyes. It's uncanny."

Ken gave Tito a cold look. Apparently, he didn't take that as a compliment. "Maybe he's my lost twin," Ken said dryly.

"I've already got a twin," Alex snapped back. And then, to make sure the guy knew he was pissed, he added, "We met on the phone last night. *'There's no one here by that name,'* " he said, imitating Ken's bland voice.

Ken raised his hands defensively. "Hey, I just do as I'm told." He glanced at Tito. "Want something to eat?"

"In a minute." Tito's eyes traveled back and forth between Alex and Ken, as if he were watching a tennis match. "I've told Ken all about you. The wild stuff we used to do when we were kids. I think he's a little jealous."

Ken came around the table and let his hand rest lightly but possessively on Tito's shoulder. Then he turned without saying anything and crossed the yard to a small outhouse at the edge of the dirt clearing.

When we were kids. As if it were another lifetime. Probably it was. Alex sat on the end of the bench, holding his head in his hands. The laundry snapped on the line behind them, and the empty soda bottle scudded across the dirt. The wind was picking up. That must be the reason he felt a massive headache coming on.

"Did you hear me?" Tito asked.

Alex turned to him blankly. "Sorry—these damned Santa Anas put me on edge. What did you say?"

Tito's smile was sweet, but sad. He rested his hand gently on Alex's arm. "I said—it should have been you."

"Should have been me—for what?" Alex's throat felt dry and hot as the Santa Ana scouring the hillside.

"Come on, Beekman. You know."

Alex let the truth pour over him, like a giant wave breaking on his shoulders. He nodded, hardly aware that he was crying. He couldn't speak.

"I'm gay," Tito said.

Alex jumped up, knocking the bench over, and paced up and down, lightly punching his fist into his palm. A cat stalked across the yard, pouncing on a dry, scudding leaf. The outhouse door banged open and shut, open and shut, as Ken walked quietly back toward the bus, avoiding them. The desert wind made each leaf stand out in detail against the sky—or maybe everything would have these sharp edges from now on, like the jagged knowledge slashing ribbons through his heart.

"Say something," Tito begged, his voice softening for the first time.

Alex swallowed. There must be words for this somewhere. Someone—Rita, perhaps, or Molly—might even know what they were. But no words came.

Alex heard the bus door close. He righted the picnic bench and sat down, holding his head again.

"Alex, look at me." Tito stood up slowly and reached for his hand, gripping it hard. "Come on, man. Don't act like you didn't know."

Alex found his voice at last, but it came out broken. "Maybe. I'm all fucked up—"

Tito sighed. "You and everyone else. My parents went bananas. This was Dad's opinion of me." Tito ran the tip of his index finger along his scarred cheek, then pointed to his leg.

Alex tasted his breakfast in his throat. "Your *father* did that to you?"

"Afraid so. My dad, the good Catholic boy, turned on his own son—slashed me with a kitchen knife, threw me down the concrete steps—"

Tito's voice broke. Alex crossed his arms tight over his chest to keep himself from embracing Tito. He was afraid if he did, their bones would break apart like twigs in the hot wind.

Tito wiped his eyes with the back of his hand. "Funny. I

111 · BLUE COYOTE

kept thinking what a waste it was. All those years you and I could have been having an even better time, if only we'd been able to admit what we knew."

"Which was—"

Tito's dark eyes glistened. "Come on, Beekman. Tell the truth! We're the same inside and out. I'm gay—and so are you."

thirteen

Was that slow moan the wind, or some horrible sound from his own body? Alex covered his ears and shut his eyes to block the noise, deny Tito's words, escape from this bad dream.

"Listen, I know it's hard." Tito's voice was far away now, hollowed out by the scouring Santa Ana. "I was a mess, at first—"

"Shut up!" Alex slammed his fist on the table. The bottle tipped over, pouring ribbons of juice through the cracks. He shot to his feet. "I'm not gay, Perone. Repeat. I. Am. Not. Gay. Never was, never will be. It's fine for you. No problem there. *Fine!* You can do what you want. I don't care—"

Tito stood slowly, gripping the table for support. He reached forward and gently, with the tip of one rough finger, wiped a tear from Alex's cheek. "Then why are you crying? Why does Ken make you so jealous?"

"Jealous?" Alex's laugh broke into a sob. "Hey, you can have whatever friends you want."

"Alex, Ken's more than a friend. I thought you guessed that."

"Whatever." Something was wrong with Alex's throat. It had closed around his tongue, like a trap sprung on the soft paw of an animal.

"Why is it all right for me to be gay—but not you?" Tito asked softly.

Alex found his voice at last, although he couldn't look at his friend. "Because—because it's not who I am, Perone.

That's all." He turned and ran before he knew he was running, tripping and stumbling over tree roots, throwing himself into the Chevy and gunning it backward out of the driveway. The station wagon lurched and jolted over rocks and potholes, the tires squealing as he wheeled onto the pavement and headed for the Pacific Coast Highway, his heart pounding.

He turned north toward Malibu, driving too fast until he realized the vibration in the steering wheel came from his own body. He pulled onto the shoulder, put on the flashers, and sat still, rubbing his arms, as if constant activity would stop his teeth from chattering, his legs from bouncing.

"Damnit!" Alex slid across the passenger's seat, pushed the door open, and vomited into the dust. He sat on the edge of the seat, his knees doubled up to his gut, until he was sure there was nothing left to bring up. Then he dug out his water bottle and swilled the bad taste from his mouth. Before he pulled out into traffic again, he twisted Tito's silver ring from his finger and shoved it into the glove box.

All the way north to Malibu he willed himself not to think. He hugged the right lane, watching every passing car, memorizing the models and plate numbers the way he and Rita used to do when they were small.

Damn. He wished he hadn't thought of his twin. The empty seat beside him made his gut feel even more scoured out. How would she feel, knowing the guy she had a crush on was gay? She'd just have to deal.

Deal? Alex laughed harshly at himself. He should talk.

His knees bounced so hard, they bumped the steering wheel. The steel door he'd kept locked up tight was threatening to open, and he couldn't stand to face the yawning hole on the other side. He pounded the dashboard, wishing he could shut off his mind, which was spinning out of control. Lights flashed in his brain—

Alex slammed on the brakes. Those lights weren't some

trick of his whacked out head, but the blue, pulsing beam of a squad car. How long had the cop been following him?

He was shaking again. Alex pulled over and rolled his window down, willing his voice to stay calm, waiting for the trooper to start the conversation. The guy wore typical cop glasses: silver mirrors that showed Alex two of himself.

"Started drinking early, didn't you kid."

"Drinking? What—"

"Wake up. You're all over the road. Or is that your idea of fun?"

"I'm sorry, officer. I didn't realize—"

"Get out and walk a straight line."

"Sure." Alex obeyed, hoping that whatever weird thing was happening to him wouldn't make him lurch from side to side. He managed to walk an easy course along the side of the highway. When he turned to come back, the trooper held up a Breathalyzer. Alex froze.

"Sir, I don't drink. I'll take the test if you want. I just threw up. Something I ate. I feel like I have a fever or something—I need to get home."

Alex couldn't tell anything about the trooper's expression behind those glasses. "Home? It's a long drive back to Vermont," the cop said, his tone a little warmer.

Alex gave him a wan smile. "Yeah. We just moved to Venice, actually."

"Then you're headed the wrong direction."

"Really?" Alex rubbed his forehead, feigning surprise. "Guess I'm really mixed up."

The trooper didn't seem amused. He checked Alex's license and registration and put the Breathalyzer away. "If you're planning to stay, you'll need a California license and plates."

"Yes, sir."

"What's your address?"

Alex told him. The trooper grunted. "I should give you a warning. That was reckless driving back there. Keep an eye on the road this time. You can turn around at the next set of lights."

Alex thanked him and waited until the trooper was out of sight before he dared reenter the slipstream of cars.

Better watch it, he told himself. You're in deep, deep trouble, man.

Hawk was right. The point break at Malibu was still outstanding. There were five guys in the water, all observing strict surfer's etiquette: waiting their turns to give each other time and space in the tube. Alex stood at the edge of the parking lot for a long time, watching and remembering. He and Tito had surfed this beach a few times when Perone first got his driver's license, the spring before Alex moved away. There was definitely a sense of being an outsider in a local crowd here, but Tito always ignored it, behaving as if he and Alex had every right to surf at Point Zero—or any of the other Malibu point breaks—which of course they did.

Today, Alex couldn't work up his nerve. He'd forgotten his wet suit, and even though the steady Santa Ana made the air hot and dry, the ocean would still be cold. Plus, the surf looked tricky. The offshore wind was doing strange things to the tubes. Alex rubbed his burning eyes. Smog hovered over the water like a sulfurous yellow pancake. He got back in the station wagon without unloading his board.

He checked his watch. Only one o'clock? This day seemed endless. He was tempted to keep driving north, to County Line Beach at Ventura, to Santa Barbara, on to Big Sur, but that was crazy. The gas tank was nearly empty, he had no cash—and Jimbo was expecting him.

Jimbo. Jesus. What was he going to say to him?

Alex headed back down the coast, stopping at a fast-food

joint for a ginger ale to settle his stomach, then kept going. This time, the tricks to empty his mind almost worked, although Tito's final words kept ringing in his skull, and when he glanced at his hand, the white band on his empty ring finger seemed to pulse. No way to escape; there were reminders everywhere. He watched the road, concentrated on his driving, played the Phish tape Klema had given him right before he left. He paid attention to signs, which was how he noticed the giant mural, painted on a building near San Vicente, showing a shark emerging from the surf. DANGER, the sign read. HUMAN INFESTED WATERS.

No wonder he had a rash. L.A. was sick. Why had he ever come back? His stomach sank as he realized his dreams—of staying here, taking off with Tito next year, making his own life away from Griswold—were just that. Dreams.

By the time he reached the pier, he was all worked up again. He put on dark glasses to hide his red eyes, locked the car, and hurried out the long boardwalk. Jimbo sat outside, his skimpy tank top revealing a paisley patchwork of skin that made Alex's eyes swim.

Jimbo squinted up at Alex. "Hey, there. Looks like you lost your best friend."

"You're right; I did." Alex glared down at his boss. "You lied to me. You knew where Perone was. You should have told me—"

Shit. He was crying again. Alex stumbled away from the shop, but Jimbo jumped up and gripped his arm. "Hold on. We've got some talking to do."

Jimbo turned the OPEN sign to CLOSED and motioned Alex inside. He pulled the shade over the door, locked it, and disappeared behind the screen, returning with a wad of tissues, which he pressed into Alex's hand. Alex took off his sunglasses, wiped his eyes, and stood in the middle of the room, feeling trapped.

Jimbo leaned against the door. "Better explain."

Alex clenched his fists. Why should he tell this creep anything? But he was too angry to keep quiet. "I found Tito in Topanga with Ken. Listen, you don't understand. The guy was my best friend." *Was*. God, it was scary how he was using the past tense. Jimbo waited, arms crossed over broad chest. "We were together every day until I moved away. Then we talked once a week. All of a sudden, in March, he disappears. Gone. No word. The family cuts me off. I come out here, find his old surfboard on the beach, think maybe he's drowned. I ask you about him, and you avoid the issue—"

Alex's chest heaved. Jimbo grabbed him by the upper arms, his dark eyes boring into him. "What did Tito say. Why is he hiding out?"

"What is this, the Inquisition?" Alex demanded. "Because his father beat him up. Obviously."

"Right. And why?"

Alex hesitated. Didn't Jimbo know? "Because he's *gay*. Big deal—"

To his astonishment, Jimbo laughed. "If you'll excuse me, it appears to be a very big deal to you."

Alex shook his head, but who was he kidding? He'd driven like a maniac, thrown up in the ditch, behaved like a fool in front of Tito. Not a big deal? Just the biggest mess in his life, that's all. Alex's legs felt rubbery. Jimbo pushed him gently toward the armchair in the waiting area. "Sit still," Jimbo said. Alex obeyed, watching while Jimbo heated water, poured it over a strange-smelling tea bag, and handed him the mug. Alex turned up his nose as he sipped the hot liquid. It was slightly bitter, but soothing.

"Ginseng tea," Jimbo said. "Now, *you* listen. I've known Perone for a while. After he got his ear pierced, he came in once in a while to talk. He knew he was safe with me. When Ken brought Tito in after the beating, he was in shock, his face slashed, his leg dangling. We didn't dare take him to a local hospital for fear his father would find him and finish the job, so we found him a place out of town, raised money to pay his bills." Jimbo pulled up a chair and sat facing Alex. "He stayed in my back room when he got out of the hospital, too weak to be alone while Ken worked. You think I should give out information that might put him at risk?"

Alex set the mug down. "But I'm his best friend—or I was. I'd never rat on him."

"How did I know that? I guessed who you were—Tito had mentioned you—but I didn't know how you'd react to his being gay. I thought you might feel betrayed; pissed off. Some people do, when they realize a close friend has been hiding something that important."

Betrayed? No, that wasn't what Alex felt. It was something far worse. He turned to face the wall and found himself staring at a red dragon with a long, curled tail and a pearl on the end of its forked tongue. If only the ugly feelings in his chest could change to jewels before they reached his mouth. "Did you call the cops on his dad?" Alex asked.

"I wanted to, but Tito wouldn't let me."

"Why not?"

"Said it would make things more dangerous. He was probably right, although I hate to see people get away with that kind of violence." Jimbo stood up, pulled on gloves, and opened the autoclave, taking out clean needles as he talked. "You searched my files, didn't you?"

Alex slumped in his chair. "You can fire me if you want. I had to do it. I couldn't figure out how else to find him."

"Never mind. I was pretty sure you'd snooped in the drawer yesterday." Jimbo's eyes warmed a little. "You put the file back in the wrong slot."

"Sorry." The dragon blurred and shifted. Alex looked away. "I didn't realize you'd done all that stuff for Tito—"

"He's a good kid. I'd do it again in a second." They heard a sharp tap on the door. Jimbo snapped the shade open and signaled that he was coming. "Next customer. Look, it's over," he said quickly. "I don't hold grudges. Whatever you do, don't give up on Tito. He needs all of us now."

Alex kept his eyes fixed on the floor. Jimbo's advice was too late. He'd already blown it with Perone. No doubt about that. He went to the bathroom to wash up, wiping his face with a wet towel. When he closed his eyes, the tar pit nightmare rushed over him. He hurried back into the room and got to work, praying that if he concentrated hard on the tasks Jimbo gave him, he could keep himself from sliding in.

The customer was a young guy who wanted a hawk soaring over a mountain pass. Jimbo asked Alex to sketch it up for him, which Alex did eagerly. Anything to keep his mind off Tito, Ken, and the gray bus.

But as the afternoon wore on, his concentration slipped. He knocked into Jimbo's fresh palette, spattering a rainbow of inks across the floor, and dropped a tray of sterilized needles. Jimbo looked exasperated. "Need to pack it in?"

"I'm sorry. I'll do better tomorrow."

An older customer waited on the table, stripped to the waist. Alex tried to clean up his spills without bumping into Jimbo, then put on his sunglasses and headed for the door. Jimbo followed him out, setting a hand on his shoulder. "We're starting a full-back tiger tattoo that will take months to complete—I'll be here until nine, at least. You can call, if you feel like talking."

"Thanks," Alex said. He was grateful for Jimbo's kindness, although he couldn't imagine what else there was to say. He'd finally found Perone—but what did it matter? Their friendship, as he had known it, was over for good.

fourteen

Alex dreaded having any kind of conversation with his father, but Chris Beekman was lost in his thoughts, and once he'd asked Alex a few perfunctory questions about his day, he didn't have much more to say.

The dry palm fronds rustled and clacked above the front walk. "Everyone was out of sorts at the studio," Chris said. "These damn Santa Anas put us on edge. Know what I mean?"

"Definitely," Alex said, glad to have an excuse for his foul mood.

It was too hot to cook, so they ate cold chicken from the fridge, and Alex offered to clean up. "Thanks," his dad said. "Otherwise I might not make that deadline. One last scene to do before we start casting tomorrow." He paused, then said, in a rush, "The director really likes the concept. They're starting to talk series—which could mean a longer stint for me out here."

"Great, Dad." Alex tried to sound enthusiastic, but it came out flat. A few days ago, he would have jumped across the kitchen to think there might be a way for him to stay. Now he pictured himself lost in endless strips of neon, wandering from beach to beach trying to find—what? He couldn't even say.

His father crossed the kitchen, then turned to look at him. "You all right? You seem awful quiet—and pale."

Alex managed a smile as he gathered up the dishes. "Guess it's the wind."

"All right." Chris wiped his glasses on his shirttail. He suddenly seemed in no hurry to get to his computer. "I'm not sure what this means for our family this fall. I wonder—" he hesitated, his eyes almost pleading. "You don't suppose you could persuade your sister and mother to move out here with us?"

Alex dumped the plastic cups into the sink. "That is *your* problem, Dad," he said angrily. "Yours and Mom's."

His father looked hurt, but he nodded. "You're right. It's just—you have more influence over Rita than anyone else in the family."

"But none over Mom," Alex reminded him.

His father's laugh was genuine. "Join the club." He disappeared into the living room.

Cleanup didn't take long. When Alex was sure his father was lost in his story, he took the portable phone into the bedroom, surprising himself by dialing Klema's number, rather than his own. Klema answered on the first ring.

"Beekman! What's up."

"Nothing much." Alex cleared his throat. "Well, actually— you can ignore my letter. I found Tito."

"No! Where?"

"It's a long story."

"So tell me. I've got all night."

Alex took a deep breath. "Okay—but it's private."

"Of course."

Slowly, without a pause, he gave Klema the whole saga, from the turtle on Tito's board to its image in the window of Jimbo's shop; his snooping in the files and the drive into Topanga. As he described the gray bus in the clearing, he thought of the way Tito's purple shirt had flapped on the line like a signal flag flashing a warning.

"Sounds like good detective work," Klema said. "You didn't need me after all." When Alex didn't say anything, Klema asked, "Is he all right?"

Alex thought a minute, remembering the sweet smile on

Tito's face when he looked at Ken, the pain in his eyes when he described the fight with his father. "Yes and no. He's been through hell. His father beat him up. Broke his leg, slashed his face, dumped him out on the street."

"Rough. What did he do, rob a bank?"

Alex struggled to keep his voice steady. "He fell in love with a guy."

Klema was quiet for an eternity. Finally he gave a low whistle. "So he's gay. No wonder."

No wonder what? Klema didn't explain. Alex went to the window, pressing his face to the screen. Out on the patio, the silver-gray eucalyptus branches whipped and turned themselves inside out in the wind.

"Beekman, you there?"

"Yeah." Alex swallowed twice. "I just feel wacked out all of a sudden."

"For sure, man. You had no idea?"

"Not really." But that was a lie, of course. Raquel was right. Alex hadn't wanted to see the obvious—for obvious reasons. "I guess there were signs, now that I think about it." Alex paced from the window to the bed to the door as memories came flooding back. The times Tito took Alex to Muscle Beach and they watched the guys flex their pecs, ignoring the girls in their bikinis. The hot night Tito wrestled Alex to the floor, their bare chests slippery with sweat, their eyes meeting in sudden shame. Tito sitting on his bed in jockey shorts while Alex forced his eyes elsewhere, away from his friend's tight, swarthy body.

"It must be weird, being such a good friend, and not knowing," Klema was saying.

Just what Jimbo had said. But of course, Alex must have known, deep inside. Who was he kidding? All the times he'd had that dream, that Tito was trying to tell him something—why couldn't he see?

Better to be blind, Alex thought.

"Beekman, you all right?"

"Yeah." Alex shifted the phone to his other ear, wiping his palm on his shorts. "I think I just blew a good friendship. I freaked out when he told me," he said, struggling to keep the pain from his voice. "I didn't handle it very well."

"Who would? That's heavy stuff, man. But you'll get over it. You've been friends a long time."

"We'll see." Alex was suddenly exhausted. He leaned his forehead against the window frame. He couldn't deal—not with any of it. He wished he could see Klema's face, so he could tell how he was taking all this. "Listen, don't mention this to Rita yet, will you? I don't know if Tito wants her to know. It may freak her out. She and Perone were close—"

"So I gathered." Klema cleared his throat. "This may sound weird—but if Rita knew Tito was gay, it could help me out."

Alex laughed for the first time all day. How crazy could things get? "What do you mean? Are you trying to date my sister?"

"Something like that. If it's all right with you."

"With *me*? Rita doesn't need my approval for anything. Hey, I wish you luck, man. You'd be good for each other."

"Thanks." Klema sounded relieved. "I'll tell her you said so."

Alex tapped his fingers on the bedside table. The steady hiss of the wind and the blank yellow walls seemed to close in even tighter. For a minute, he wished he were back in Griswold, sitting under the big broken maple at Klema's place, talking about other things. And damn—he did miss Rita.

There was a knock on Alex's door and his father poked his head in. "I need to use the modem."

Alex nodded, then turned his back quickly, hoping his

father couldn't tell he'd been crying. "Gotta go, Klema. My dad wants the phone."

"Okay. Just tell me, quickly—does this mean you'll be back soon? The guys on the team were wondering."

"I'm not sure. It all depends—things here are confused. I'll call you again soon."

"Sure. I understand. Hang in there, dude."

Alex said good-bye and called to his father to let him know the phone was free. He pulled out his sketch pad and tried to draw, but nothing looked right. He was scratching out his third attempt at a dragon when he suddenly felt his father's presence in the doorway. His left hand slipped, spoiling the drawing. "Damnit, Dad—you surprised me."

"Sorry." His father came into the room without being invited and sat on the end of the bed. "Were you talking with a friend from L.A.?"

"No. That was Klema. In Vermont."

His father's short legs swung above the rug. "Shouldn't you make an effort to call some people here? I'm sure some of Rita's friends would love to hear from you—"

"Jesus!" Alex jumped up, putting as much space as possible between them. "Will you lay off the girl stuff? I told you before: Stop hounding me!"

Chris slumped backward on his elbows, exasperated. "Alex, you're much too sensitive about this. I'm not trying to get you a date. I just thought you used to enjoy some of her friends—and you seem so lonely."

"I am," Alex admitted softly. He stood at the window, twisting the cord on the venetian blind. No matter what he did, this day circled back around to the same damned topic, like a crazy spiral gone mad. When his father's arm slipped gently around his waist Alex slowly leaned into him, biting his lip to keep from crying. If only they could talk—but Alex knew it was hopeless.

"I'm sorry, Alex. I know I don't always say the right thing—" his father began, and then froze.

Alex tensed at the same instant, as alert as a cat. They looked at each other. "What's that smell?" they said in unison.

"Something's burning." His father bolted from the room.

They rushed through the living room, circled the kitchen, threw open the other bedroom door, looked into closets, sniffing. Nothing. Alex yanked the sliding door open. "It's outside."

They stood on the patio, sniffing the air like dogs. The air was acrid, tasting of smoke. Doors slammed up and down the street, and in the distance, beginning as a lonesome wail, building to a fever pitch of screaming, the sirens began. "A brush fire—I'd better call the studio. That canyon is vulnerable." Chris ran for the kitchen.

Alex held on to the fence to steady himself. No question about the sirens. They came from the south and were headed north on the Pacific Coast Highway.

"The studio's safe," his father called from the kitchen. "The fire's at the top of Topanga—and there's another one farther east, in the San Gabriels."

"No," Alex whispered, hardly aware he spoke out loud. "Not Topanga. Not Tito—please."

fifteen

Alex stuffed his bike helmet, gloves, and a windbreaker into his backpack and ran for the kitchen, nearly colliding with his father in the doorway. "I need the car," he said, trying to push past.

"Hold it," his father said, blocking his way. "You're not going to that fire."

Alex bounced on his toes. A bomb ticked inside him, about to explode, but he forced himself to speak calmly. "You think I'm crazy, Dad? I left my wallet full of cash at Jimbo's—gotta run before he closes. I won't be long." Alex gave his father a quick, sideways hug which put him off guard just long enough to let him swipe the keys off the counter and slide past.

He wrestled his bike into the back of the car, glancing toward the kitchen. There was no sign of his father in the window, but the door slammed as Alex jumped into the front seat. "Alex, wait!" his father cried. Alex revved the engine to cover his father's voice, shifted quickly into reverse, and took off down the road without looking back.

He made himself drive slowly until he'd turned the first corner where he wheeled out onto Ocean Boulevard and floored the Chevy until it rattled. The blood pounded in his head, and he seemed to hit every red light in town. Alex pounded the steering wheel. "Change, goddamnit! Change!" he shrieked at the lights.

Tito and Ken would get out, wouldn't they? The top of Topanga was pretty far from the bus. Surely they'd make a run for it. But in what? Alex couldn't remember seeing a car there.

Could they drive the bus? Doubtful. Alex had a sudden, vivid picture of Tito alone, limping away from the fire on his bum leg. He smashed the accelerator to the floor, running two yellow lights, then a red.

He switched the radio to an all-news station, which basically told him what his father had already heard, but also reported that a third fire had broken out in the San Gabriels.

"Jesus." Alex finally reached the California Incline, caught the left turn signal just in time, and booked it down the hill to the Pacific Coast Highway.

Traffic streamed north on the PCH, as if a giant magnet were sucking everyone toward the fires. It was a clear evening, with a nearly full moon rising in the dusk. The smoke formed a dense, horizontal cloud that stretched from the mountains out over the Pacific. Every once in a while, red flames came licking over the top of the dark ridgeline, then disappeared. The scream of sirens seemed to come from all directions. Like the rest of the cars, Alex pulled over every few minutes to let another yellow engine rumble past. The trucks came from Marina del Ray, San Pedro, Culver City, Los Angeles. He clenched the steering wheel and pulled into the slipstream of each engine, as if the truck's power could draw him along at a faster pace. When he reached the canyon, the entrance was blocked by a police barricade and a couple of state troopers wearing white flak helmets. Just as he'd expected.

A swarthy cop with a barrel chest leaned into Alex's window. "No one's going in," he said, before Alex could even begin the story he'd concocted.

"Please, officer. My brother's stuck up there," Alex protested. "He's got a broken leg and no way to get out—"

"That's what the rescue trucks are for. They'll find him. Where's he live?"

Alex gave him the address. The cop made a quick note on a handheld pocket computer and waved Alex off. "Move it, you're in the way." Alex backed up, maneuvering into a U-turn as a mass exodus of cars, vans, and pickup trucks, laden with people and possessions, poured out of the canyon, their drivers glancing quickly over their shoulders as if the fire were right behind them.

Alex parked on the shoulder and pulled out his bike. As he strapped on his helmet, a car pulled up beside him and the driver got out to tighten the ropes on a chair tied to the roof. "How far down has the fire come?" Alex asked.

The man glanced at him, obviously annoyed by the question. His face was streaked with soot. "About halfway," he said. "It's a bitch. Taking everything in its path. I doubt we'll see our house in the morning." He turned away, his shoulders shaking with sudden sobs.

"Sorry." Alex felt like an idiot. He strapped on his helmet and gloves, rode to the canyon entrance, and wheeled into the shadows away from the headlights, waiting for his chance to get past the cops. It didn't take long. The big trooper leaned into the window to argue with a woman who was screaming hysterically about rescuing her dog, while the other turned to talk to a man coming out of the canyon, his Jeep Cherokee loaded with kids and furniture. Alex tucked his head and pedaled hard around the end of the barrier, keeping his light out until he'd rounded the first corner and headed up the hill.

The road was much steeper than he'd realized. Soon his lungs burned and his legs screamed out for rest, but he kept going, hugging the shoulder, watching every set of headlights for the gray bus. What a fool he was! If only he'd stayed to talk with Tito. Or called him before he left. He had no idea where Tito worked, how he spent his time. Maybe he and Ken were out somewhere partying, or having dinner, or working some boring job—and here he was, frying his lungs to get there— and do what? Save them? Who was he kidding? On a bike, no less.

About two miles up the hill, an old Ford pickup braked suddenly behind him, catching him in the full glare of its headlights. The driver called out, "Hey, dude! I almost hit you. Want a ride?"

Alex jumped off his bike, gasping for breath. "Sure. How far you going?"

"A few more miles, if they let me. My place is near the top. Come on, throw that thing in the back. I've got to hustle."

Alex set his bike in the truck's bed, careful not to let it fall on a sweet little triple-fin board resting against the cab, and jumped into the front seat. "Thanks for stopping."

"No problem. Neither one of us should be here, but I figure your reasons must be as good as mine."

Alex glanced at his rescuer. He couldn't see much in the dark, but the guy appeared to be in his early twenties. His long curly hair was slicked back and he wore a half wet suit pulled down around his waist. "You just come from the beach?" Alex asked.

"Yeah. I stayed too long—I was surfing Point Zero, out at Malibu, when I saw the smoke. Ever worked that point break?"

"I was out there today looking around," Alex said. "I didn't have time to go in."

"So come back soon, dude," the surfer said. "You should have stayed—but shit, I wish I'd left earlier. Those sons of bitches who started this fire—if they've burned up my boards, they're dead." He pressed harder on the accelerator, and the truck's engine whined. The old Ford nearly lost it on the curves, its long bed fishtailing out.

The surfer laughed, then tossed him an admiring look. "You're crazy, dude, pedaling up here in the dark."

Alex laughed. "I know. I couldn't get past the cops with my car. How'd you manage?"

"Fast talk. One of the troopers is a weekend surfer."

"Seriously?"

"Yeah. He's tough: that barrel-chested guy with the shades. Surfed the Pipeline last year. He looked the other way while I cruised past. So, where you going?"

"Weasel Creek Road. That's where my buddy is."

The surfer laughed. "And you're going to rescue him on a bike. Get real."

Alex shrugged. "He has a broken leg and no car. If it's dicey, we'll hitch a ride out."

The surfer downshifted on the next corner, then floored it again. Alex grinned in spite of himself, gripping the door handle. His adrenaline was pumping. How long since he'd been out on the edge like this? Too long. But this was definitely a crazy way to get your kicks.

"Weasel Creek is beyond my turn," the surfer said. "You'll have to excuse me, dude, but I can't drive you all the way up there—my roommates will kill me if I don't get home in time. We've got some serious stereo equipment to rescue—not to mention a complete stash of sticks."

He went on to describe all his boards, and Alex only half listened, annoyed with the guy's bragging. Who cared about his triple scag? What about the people, and their houses? Alex watched the steady stream of traffic pour down the canyon. It was almost impossible to see the make or size of a vehicle until they'd gone by, especially since the surfer was pushing the Ford for all it was worth. If the bus passed, he'd probably miss it. With the window down, the smoke made their eyes smart. Helicopters chopped and chattered above them, punctuating the shrieking of sirens. Alex's shirt stuck to the plastic seat of the truck. His throat was dry, and his legs bounced so nervously that his knees kept hitting the glove box, but he couldn't help it.

A few more fire trucks squealed past them going up, then some small pickups with flashing lights and a couple of station wagons with portable lights on top. "The serious firefighters," the surfer told Alex. "Those guys are so psyched when there's a burn—my dad claims they start them just for the rush they get when they fight the bastards."

"Come on."

"I know, it's pretty far-fetched—one of my old man's wild theories." He slammed on the brakes. "Sorry, dude; this is my turn. Good luck. And hey—don't mess with the fire. It can do a mean long jump." He pulled over quickly, waiting only a few seconds for Alex to lift out his bike before peeling around the corner and out of sight. Alex climbed back on his bike, grateful for his gloves; the handlebars were warm. It was scary how bright the road was now that the top of the mountain was engulfed in flames, dancing along the ridgeline.

It was less than a mile to Weasel Creek, but the road was steep. Alex tucked his head, pushing himself forward, ignoring his protesting legs and lungs. As he drew close, he felt as if he were coming into a war zone. Engines rumbled, searchlights flashed, and voices called out to each other in the darkness. Sometimes a sweeping light caught a man or a woman hosing down a roof, legs braced wide on the sloping shingles.

Weasel Creek Road was closed off, and the burly man at the entrance wasn't interested in Alex's story. "I don't care if your *mother's* in there, you're not going," the man snapped. "Can't you see? The fire's jumped the highway twice up above, and it's headed this way."

Alex looked up the canyon. Fires were erupting all over the place, as if someone were launching missiles from above. "You seen a gray bus drive out of here?" Alex asked.

"Nothing's come down since I got here twenty minutes ago. Now beat it, kid. The trucks will be here in a minute. We got a bunch of houses to save."

Alex turned around, coasted down the hill until he was out of the man's sight, and then locked his bike to a big live oak tree near a road sign. He slunk into the chaparral, keeping to the dark shadows, stumbling and tripping in the brush. He thought about rattlers slithering away to avoid the fires, about poison oak on his bare legs, but he kept going, wishing the coyote would appear to lead him to safety. The coyote was probably the only one in the canyon who knew his way out of here.

Alex came out of the brush on the other side of the barrier and ran down the road in the dark. The smoky air burned his lungs and made his eyes smart. The fire hissed and crackled, devouring everything in its path, looming above him like the red dragon on the wall of Jimbo's tattoo shop.

A car bumped toward him. Alex darted to the side, but he'd been caught in the flare of the headlights. The driver stopped and rolled her window down. It was a woman his mother's age, with a bunch of small kids in the back. "Get in," she said. "It's not safe up here."

Alex shook his head. "I'm almost home," he said. "I'll be okay."

She hesitated, then one of her kids began to bawl and she hit the accelerator, lurching past him.

Alex kept running, his breath coming in sobs. The fire was on the hillside above him now, and he felt as if he were on the soccer field, dribbling a ball toward the goal while teammates yelled, "Man on! Man on!" about the hot opponent breathing down his back. He nearly banged into Tito's tilted mailbox as he turned into the driveway, which was no longer in the dark. The fire streaked the night sky and raced toward the clearing like something alive. In the chaparral, scrub oak bushes burst into sudden flame as if they'd been doused in gasoline, their oily sap feeding the flames. Alex rounded the corner and stood trembling, poised on the balls of his feet, about to make a dash for the darkened bus when sparks began raining on the clearing and the wind dropped a fireball into the eucalyptus tree.

"Tito!" Alex screamed. He ran forward as a line of flames licked across the bus roof like a snaking, red tongue. The peeling paint around the rusty stovepipe began to smoke. Alex pounded on the locked door, but it wouldn't budge. "Tito! Ken! Are you in there?" The air was suddenly too hot and thick to breathe. The fire lit the chaparral all around him, blackening it within seconds. "Tito!" Alex called again. The back of the bus erupted in flames. Alex grabbed Tito's T-shirt from the line and held it over his nose and mouth, rubbing his singed face. He fled with the fire at his back, not daring to turn around for fear the sight of it would make him fall into its path.

He repeated Tito's name with every pounding step. Tito couldn't die. Not now. What if he never knew how Alex felt about him?

When he reached the road, Alex felt the rumble of fire engines through the hot soles of his shoes. He stepped into the path of their headlights, desperately waving the shirt to flag them down. The driver braked and swerved to the side of the road.

"There's a bus on fire, down that driveway," Alex cried, pointing wildly in the direction of the clearing. "My friend might be in there—"

"Okay, kid, we'll check," the driver said. "How the hell did you get up here, anyway?" Without waiting for an answer, he turned to his squawking radio and spoke into it. "There's a kid up here, needs to be driven out. Weasel Creek. Yeah, we'll keep him in the pickup until you get here." He threw the radio down and pointed to the smaller truck behind him. "Get in the cab with Leon." When Alex started to protest, he barked, "Do as I say. We'll see about your friend. Now move it."

Alex ran for the pickup behind him and climbed into the cab to wait for the cruiser while the fire truck lurched into Tito's driveway. The squad car came in less than a minute, popping its bubblegum light. Alex climbed in front and sat facing sideways, watching the flames engulf the hillside as they careened along the switchbacks. The trooper passed a station wagon on a curve and flagged it down, ordering Alex out. "Take this kid, will you, ma'am?" the cop asked the woman driving.

She nodded. "Get in back." She was crying, and so were most of the kids, except for a scrappy girl with a runny nose who announced matter-of-factly, as Alex climbed in beside her, "Your face looks gross."

Alex ignored her, holding himself tight with his arms to control the shaking. His forehead felt hot and seared, but he didn't dare touch it. Halfway down the hill, he remembered his bike, locked to the tree. He didn't say anything. The woman was driving too fast to stop. When she pulled up at the roadblock, Alex stumbled out the door without even thanking her. He dodged through the crowd of reporters and photographers that had gathered at the barricades, running for the Chevy.

Alex drove south without thinking, and found himself parking at the pier before he even knew he'd planned to. He hustled out to the end, gasping for breath, and stood for a few seconds behind the crowd near the restaurant deck. The viewers were exclaiming over the distant fires like spectators at a fireworks display. Alex waited long enough to watch flames erupt in the middle of one darkened mountain, and then staggered into Jimbo's, pushing the door open and falling into a plastic chair near the window. The shop seemed empty, but then he heard water running in the bathroom and Jimbo came out, peeling rubber gloves from his hand. He did a double take when he saw Alex.

"Beekman? Jesus Christ!" He cupped Alex's chin with his big hand. "You get caught in the fire? Damn. Your eyebrows are gone. It singed your hair, too."

Alex closed his eyes, too tired to care. When he opened them, Jimbo stood in front of him holding a glass of water and two aspirin. "Take these," he said, "and then we'll clean you up."

Alex sat still while Jimbo washed his face with the same green disinfectant he used before giving a tattoo. He let him clip the burned ends from his hair and swab his eyebrows with ointment. When he was done, Jimbo said gently, "You went to Topanga. Did you find him?"

Alex shook his head. "I tried to get into the bus, but it was locked. Then the fire caught me. What if he was asleep in there?" The shaking started again, and Alex crossed his arms over his chest.

Jimbo sat next to him, his arm around his shoulder. "No way he'd sleep through that. Teams of people went through early this evening, evacuating everyone. I saw it on television."

Alex slumped against the big man, hoping he was right. "But where would he go? He's got no place—"

"He's got Ken," Jimbo said. "They'll figure something out. Crash in someone's dorm room, maybe."

Alex couldn't hold the tears back. He let them come while Jimbo kept a tight grip around his shoulders, patting his back to soothe him. Something foul rose in his mouth, as sour as the smell of his singed flesh, and he knew he was tasting jealousy. For the first time since he'd jumped into the Chevy at the house, he let himself view the fantasy that had driven him into the canyon: Alex coming on Tito, alone, rescuing him somehow, leading him out of the fire—and Tito throwing his sturdy arms around him in gratitude. *It should have been you,* Tito had said. But it wasn't. It was Ken. If Tito had escaped the fire—and Alex was sure he had; surely Jimbo was right—then it was Ken who had rescued him. Ken whom Tito chose, in part, because he reminded him of Alex.

Ken is gay, Alex reminded himself. So is Tito. That's why they're together. Wake up.

Crazy thoughts careened back and forth inside his skull. Alex pressed his fists to his temples.

"Want to talk?" Jimbo asked quietly.

Alex wiped his face with his shirttail. "I was an asshole—treated Tito like shit—"

"Hey." Jimbo let go of Alex and moved his chair around so they were facing each other. "Listen. When Tito stayed here, he talked about you."

Alex finished his water. "What did he say?"

"Not a whole lot. Just that you were a special friend. Like I said earlier, he never told me your name, but when you came in looking for him, I figured you were probably the one—he said you were tall and handsome, with navy eyes." Jimbo's expression was steady and kind. "Tito will still be your friend. He's just confused."

Aren't we all, Alex thought. He sighed and looked over at Jimbo. "Sorry I made such a mess today."

Jimbo's smile showed white teeth behind his dark beard. "You *are* a challenging employee, I'll grant you that. How about a little rest while I clean up."

"I should help you," Alex protested, but when Jimbo led him into the booth, he sank onto the tattoo table as if it were his own bed. He was out cold before Jimbo even turned off the light behind the screens.

sixteen

Alex dreamed that sirens were chasing him down the Pacific Coast Highway into a wall of flame, and woke to the shrilling of the phone, followed by Jimbo's smooth, low voice saying, "Yes, yes. He's right here. Hold on."

Alex nearly fell off the narrow platform, forgetting where he was. He sat up slowly. Every muscle in his body ached, as if he'd just finished the first day of soccer practice after months away from the field. He blinked up at Jimbo, trying to remember what had happened. The stocky man cupped his hand under Alex's elbow, helping him to his feet like an invalid. "Your dad's on the phone."

Alex took the call by the window, staring, in a daze, at the crowds of people streaming past, not sure if he'd been asleep for minutes or days. "Hey, Dad—"

His father's voice was as tight as a coiled spring. "Where the hell have you been? It's nearly midnight."

Alex glanced at his watch. Damn. He was royally screwed this time. "I'll explain when I get home—"

Chris Beekman was fuming so that Alex could barely understand him. "Tell that man you work for I expect a good explanation for what goes on at his shop."

"Dad, calm down! It's nothing to do with Jimbo. He got me out of a tough spot. Are you home?"

"Where else would I be? You've got the car. I've been frantic for the last hour, trying to track you down. I was afraid you'd gone to the fire."

"I did." His father sucked in his breath, and Alex said

quickly, before he could explode again, "Relax, Dad, I'm fine. See you in a few minutes."

He set the phone in its cradle and looked at Jimbo. The man's dark eyes were full of sympathy. "Big trouble, huh?"

"No kidding. He claims he's coming to talk to you tomorrow."

"I can handle it. Just get yourself home safely."

Alex went to the long mirror and peered at his face. His forehead was raw and blistered, as if he'd spent all day in the sun, and his singed eyebrows gave his eyes a lost, sunken look.

"You'll never win a beauty contest now," Jimbo teased. "Come on. I'll walk you to your car." He followed Alex out the door, shutting off the lights and locking up behind them. They stood at the railing a minute, looking north. Smoke billowed from the mountains out to sea for miles, a dense, rolling cloud hunkering over the Pacific like a dragon, its tail nearly swallowing the moon. "That would be a pretty sight, if you didn't know what caused it," Jimbo said, shaking his head. "They ought to string up the guy who set this one."

They walked in silence along the pier. Just past the restaurant, Alex heard a low whistle and turned to see Jason, the tall muscular man who had come in for a tattoo on Alex's first day at work. "Hey, Alex." Jason's voice was deep and melodic. His blue eyes cruised over Alex's body, widening when he took in his burned face. "What goes on in that shop?" he asked.

Alex looked away quickly, his palms sweaty with nervousness.

"Bug off, Jase," Jimbo said. "Alex got hurt in the fire."

"Sorry, guys," Jason called after them. "No harm meant."

When they were out of earshot, Jimbo asked, "He come onto you the other day?"

"Sort of." Alex was embarrassed, although Jimbo sounded as if it was no big deal.

"Just ignore him," Jimbo said. "He does that with any-one he considers good-looking, gay or straight. But he's all right, as long as you're clear from the beginning."

At this point, Alex didn't feel clear about anything. They walked in silence to the Chevy, and when Jimbo said good-bye, Alex put out his hand and shook Jimbo's hard. "Thanks for tonight," he said. "I appreciate it."

"Anytime. Think you'll feel like working tomorrow? I got a bunch of walk-ins earlier who claim to be coming back in the afternoon."

"I'll be here. For sure."

Alex climbed into the car and searched through his tapes, looking for something soothing, and picked the *Strength in Numbers* album Klema had given him for the cross-country drive. He sat still with the engine running, listening to Bela Fleck's cool opening banjo chords, the delicate haunting phrases somewhere between bluegrass and jazz. If only Rita were here. But even his sister, who knew most of his secrets, couldn't help him with this one.

He checked the date on his watch. July first. The rest of the summer stretched out ahead of him, as empty and dark as the Pacific pounding against the slick pylons under the pier. And if he didn't do what he needed to, the flames lodged in his chest might erupt, consuming him with the vengeance of the Topanga fire.

His father was waiting impatiently on the steps outside the kitchen door, and his expression changed from anger to horror when he saw Alex's face under the light. "My God! What happened to you!"

"I got singed." Alex pushed past him, dropping Tito's shirt on the kitchen table. "It's nothing serious. My hair will grow back." He headed straight for the fridge, but his father grabbed his elbow. "Let me look at you." Alex held still, his eyes closed, while his father examined his face. "I think we'd better get you to a doctor—"

"Dad, I'm fine." Alex struggled to keep his temper. "Jimbo cleaned me up with disinfectant soap and ointment. He said I'd be all right in a few days."

"Who is this Jimbo guy, some kind of medicine man?"

Alex grinned. "You could say that."

His father's jowly cheeks sagged. "Tomorrow I'm taking you to work so I can meet him myself. Tonight I want the full explanation."

They sat at the kitchen table. His father drank a beer while Alex downed a tall glass of orange juice and ate a heaping bowl of cereal. He was suddenly ravenous. Chris peppered him with questions, and Alex answered with as little information as possible, telling his father only that he had a friend in the canyon with no radio or TV, and he'd gone to see if he could help him save his place.

"Look, don't tell me I was stupid," he said, anticipating his father's next attack. "I already figured that out. I forgot how fast brush fires move, how they jump over things."

"How did you get past the barricades?"

"On my bike, when the cops weren't looking." Alex was proud of this move, but he didn't expect his father to praise him. Only someone like Klema or Tito would appreciate the thrill of the adrenaline rush that had pushed him up that hill. Alex twisted Tito's shirt in his hands. "I know I screwed up. My bike is still in the canyon, locked to a tree. Probably burned to a crisp."

His father sniffed and went to the window, closing it tight, but the kitchen still smelled smoky. "I'm the one who's rank," Alex said. "I'll take a shower in a minute."

Chris Beekman stood with his back to him for so long that Alex grew anxious. Finally he burst out, "Come on, Dad, what's my punishment? Let's get it over with, okay?"

But when his father turned around, his eyes were sorrow-ful, not angry, which made Alex wary. Chris leaned against the fridge, his arms crossed over his pot belly. "I don't get it, Alex. You're leading a secret life here. You say you haven't called any of your old friends, yet I keep feeling you're sneaking around to see people. You come home with your face scorched and a vague story that doesn't really fit. You've obviously been upset about something ever since we arrived." He wiped his face with his hand. "I feel as if I don't know you anymore. How can I help you if I don't know what's going on?"

Alex scooped a handful of ice from the freezer, stalling for time. "Gee, Dad. Heavy-duty." He ran an ice cube over his singed eyebrows to cool them. "I'm not sure I need help right now. If I do, I'll let you know."

"Great, Alex. That's just great." His father stalked up and down the kitchen, knocking into chairs, slamming his fists randomly against the cupboards. Alex felt afraid. He'd never seen him like this. Was everything in his life going to be out of control from now on?

Chris suddenly whirled to face him. "You're going to have to let me call your mother."

"Fine. What is she supposed to do? Fly out here to check my burns?"

Chris sat down, pulling his chair close so their knees almost touched. "She'll probably tell me I should send you home."

Alex laughed; he couldn't help it. "*Home?* You must be joking, Dad. Where is that, anyway?"

His father gripped the edge of the table. "What is that sup-posed to mean?"

"Just that I've moved so many times, I don't know where my home is. Do you?"

His father's anger seemed to deflate slowly, like a punc-tured soccer ball. "No," he admitted. "I guess I don't."

Alex hadn't meant to make his father feel bad, and now he didn't know what else to say. He tossed the orange juice carton at the trash, missed, and got up to retrieve it. He glanced at his father. Chris had put his glasses back on, making his eyes look bigger.

"Let's not fight about this. If you stay here, you have to convince me your behavior will change, that's all. Otherwise, I don't feel safe, leaving you alone while I'm working."

"For Christ's sake, Dad! I'm not a baby."

"Then act your age," his father snapped.

Alex sighed. "I *am,* Dad. I'm seventeen."

To Alex's surprise, his father laughed, breaking the tension in the room. "That's fair. But then, I suppose I'm behaving like a middle-aged parent who needs to know he can trust his son."

"How do I know I can trust *you?*" Alex demanded.

His father rubbed his chin. "What do you mean?"

"If I tell you what's going on, how do I know you won't blab it all over the place?"

His father's gaze was as steady as his voice. "Because I'm not that kind of man," he said firmly.

Alex bit his lip. He knew, in his heart, that his father was telling the truth. He clasped Tito's shirt to his chest to give him strength as he took his first step out on the high wire. "You're right, Dad; there's some weird stuff going on. It's about Tito." His father raised an eyebrow, but didn't say anything. "When we were still in Vermont, I heard that he'd disappeared. It took me a while, but I finally found him yesterday, in Topanga. That's why I went there tonight. He's been—" Alex stopped. His father's eyes were full of questions. "Dad, promise you won't say anything about this—even to Mom?"

"I already said yes." His father sounded exasperated. Beads of sweat broke out on his forehead.

"Dad, Tito's been disowned by his parents."

Chris stared. "Why? What did he do?"

"He didn't really *do* anything. He just happens to be gay, that's all." Alex hurried on before his father could respond. "His parents freaked when he told them, kicked him out of the house."

Chris Beekman began to cough. He went to the sink, ran a glass of water, and swallowed it down, wiping his eyes.

"You okay, Dad?"

His father nodded. "Go on," he said, when he could speak. "Finish the story."

The dismay in his father's eyes made Alex's heart beat ninety miles an hour. "I thought Tito might be trapped in the canyon. He's got a bad leg and he was living in a bus up there. I couldn't get into the bus before the fire came, so I'm not sure he got out. I'm not going back to Vermont until I'm sure he's safe."

He waited while his father wiped his glasses for what seemed like the thousandth time. Finally, Chris's sad eyes met his own. "Let me make sure I heard you right. Tito Perone is *gay?* Is this some kind of joke?"

"Not to some people." Alex's voice shook. "Why, do you think it's funny?"

"Of course not. I'm just—well, I'm shocked, that's all. Aren't you?"

The room was quiet. Distant sirens wailed to the north. Finally Alex said, "No, Dad. I'm not."

His father blinked, like someone who's come out of the movie theater into a bright afternoon. "I'm sorry, Alex. I don't know what to say. Everything's moving a little too fast for me."

Tell me about it, Alex thought. He felt let down, deflated— and utterly disappointed in his father. But what did he expect? "Aren't you going to tell me what you think?"

"About Tito being gay? I'm not sure what to say—except

that I understand why his parents might be upset—"

Alex was pacing again, socking his fists against his thigh. "I see. So it's okay for Mr. Perone to slash Tito's face with a kitchen knife, push him out the door, kick him down the concrete steps, break his leg in two places—"

His father stood up and grabbed Alex by the elbows. "What are you telling me?"

"The *truth,* Dad!" To keep from crying, Alex forced the wall back up inside him, making it as solid and heavy as the dam he'd built with Klema in the spring. This wall had protected him ever since he was small and realized he was different from everyone else—even his twin.

Alex started to wipe his face with Tito's shirt, then cringed, forgetting his burns. "Forget we had this conversation," he said softly. "I'm beat." He left the room, but his father followed close behind.

"Alex, wait. I'm not sure—"

He guessed what his father was about to say. "Not sure you want me seeing Tito? Well, don't worry. I blew it so badly when he told me the news, I'll probably never hear from him again."

Alex shut the door gently but firmly in his father's face. He stood there for a long minute, his hands braced against the handle, until he heard his father's bare feet pad away on the wood floor. Feeling like a coward, Alex pushed in the button to lock the door.

Damn, Alex thought. Why the hell did I ever bring that up? But of course, he knew the answer to that one.

Something was different when he woke the next morning. Alex pulled the curtains and peered out. The city was swathed in fog, and the wind was coming off the sea. The Santa Ana had returned to the desert.

He dressed as slowly and carefully as an old man, every muscle screaming with pain. His face was already peeling, and his eyes seemed naked and bugged out without his eyebrows. He plastered his burns with zinc oxide, then studied his hair in the mirror, wishing he had Rita's barber scissors to trim the scorched ends. What the hell. He didn't care how he looked today.

He decided to eat lunch, rather than breakfast, and found a note from his father on the kitchen table:

> *"Alex—I'm sorry about the way I reacted last night. I was worried about you—and still am. I know I don't express it very well, but I do care about you. I'll come back to drive you to work at two-thirty, unless you need to see a doctor beforehand. . . . Dad."*

Alex ate a turkey sandwich, then a peanut butter sandwich, then an orange and a banana, and finally his energy level began to rise, even though there was still a gnawing in his gut that had nothing to do with hunger.

If his team felt this stiff after soccer practice, a coach would have no sympathy, just tell his players to get out there and hustle some more. So Alex made himself walk to the beach, jog a little way on the sand, walk, then jog again, then stretch, until some of the kinks actually eased up. The cool fog was secretive and comforting and the smell of smoke was gone.

Back at the house, Alex switched on the TV to the news channel, where he learned that the Topanga fire was nearly out but the eastern blaze was still burning in the San Gabriels. And the surfer dude was right—some volunteer firefighter had been arrested for arson. "Unreal," Alex said. The world was too weird to be believed.

He did a wash, putting Tito's shirt in with his grubby clothes, and cleaned up the kitchen. At two-fifteen, he was dressed in a black T-shirt and shorts, ready for work, and was about to go outside to wait for his father when the phone rang.

It was Tito.

Alex walked into the living room with the phone, sweat breaking out all over his body. "Perone. You're all right?"

Tito's voice broke. "I'm safe. That's about all I can say. I just talked to Jimbo—he told me you came to the bus last night."

"Yeah. I got fixated on the idea that you were trapped up there. I rode my bike into the canyon, hitched a ride—scorched my face. I was afraid—" Alex's voice caught. He breathed deep to steady himself. "I was afraid you might be inside. I freaked out."

Tito was quiet a long time. Finally he said, "Biking into a fire. Sounds like the old Beekman: a crazy man. I can't believe you did that for me— I wasn't sure if we were still friends."

"Neither was I."

They were both quiet. Then Tito said, "The bus is a mess. But it's not completely gone—the trucks got there in time."

Alex was relieved. His efforts had paid off. "If I could have hosed it down—but I was too late. The fire jumped on me like some big cat. I was scared shitless. And the cops were about to kill me for messing around in the fire—I wouldn't move until they promised to go in there and find you."

"You're the one who told them about the bus?"

"Yeah."

"Thanks. You did better than Ken and me. We were both at work—by the time we heard what was happening, they'd closed the canyon. You must have used some cool maneuvers, to get up in there."

"I was moving fast." Alex smiled, proud of himself. "Where are you now?"

"With Raquel, at the club. She gave me your number. So, you ready to talk?"

"Definitely." His heart hammered. He heard a car outside and peered through the venetian blinds. "Damn. My dad's

here. He's going to take me to work. When can we get together?"

"Tonight," Tito said. "What time are you done?"

"Around eight."

"I'll come to Jimbo's. Wait for me there."

Tito hung up without saying good-bye. Alex stared at the
phone a minute, then set it down, wiping his sweaty palms on
his shorts. He felt as if he'd jumped into a fast car where someone else was driving. He was sitting back, calmly watching his
world come unglued. So why in hell was he so excited?

seventeen

Jimbo was great with Alex's dad. He gave him a tour of the shop, including a full description of the way he sterilized needles and disposed of them after each use. He showed him all the inks, and praised Alex's work. "Your son's a quick study," Jimbo told Chris, "and he's artistic. I appreciate your letting him work here. Some parents wouldn't be so tolerant. Not everyone understands that tattooing is an art—and that we're working hard to keep it safe."

Jimbo was smart, to make his father think he was being liberal. Alex shot his boss a grateful smile behind his father's back. Chris stayed to watch them set up for their first customer and before he left, asked if he could come back to take some notes. "I'm working on a script for a new TV series. There's a guy in the story with tattoos all over his back. I'd like to make sure we portray things accurately."

"You're a writer?" Jimbo asked. "Alex didn't tell me that. Sure, anytime—it's good public relations for the shop, maybe an interesting angle for you."

Chris squeezed Alex's shoulder. Alex smiled; Jimbo had passed the test. "What time shall I pick you up?" his father asked.

Alex hesitated. "I've got a ride—but don't worry, I won't be late," he added quickly. "If I'm going to be after eleven, I'll call you."

His father frowned, then said reluctantly, "All right. As long as you're finished fighting fires with the L.A. Fire Department."

"Yeah, I'm done. Thanks, Dad." He ushered his father out

the door, proud of him for being cool about last night, for not grounding him or taking the car away. And no mention of Tito—thank God.

Jimbo winked at him. "I do all right?"

"Perfect. He should be off my back about this stuff, at least."

The first customer was a young woman who came in with her boyfriend. She asked for a blue and purple Pegasus on her upper thigh. Jimbo set up the screens to give her privacy and sent Alex to help the boyfriend choose his tattoo from the designs on the wall. He picked something nerdy: a dancing devil in diapers, carrying a pitchfork. Alex wanted to warn him he'd probably regret it in a few years, but Jimbo had told him, his first night on the job, that you don't challenge the customer's choice.

The shop was busy all afternoon and into the evening, and a few people asked Alex to help them with original designs. He was glad for the distractions. Whenever business slowed, his nerves buzzed like the motor whining behind the parchment screens.

At eight o'clock, Jimbo was still trying to transform an old, boring tattoo of a dagger into an intricate floral design on a pudgy man's arm. Alex stood beside his boss, holding the palette of inks, occasionally helping him swab the tattoo clean. He felt like an operating room nurse with his surgeon.

The chain of bells jangled when the door opened. Alex's heart raced as he watched Tito from behind the screen. His friend was dressed in a black tank top, faded jeans, and heavy boots. His hair hung loose on his shoulders; bright links of coral around his neck accentuated his tan. When he smiled, Alex caught a glimpse of the cocky kid who had surfed on his lunch tray so long ago.

"Hey, Perone." Alex came out from behind the screen.

Tito's smile disappeared. "Jesus, Beekman. You didn't tell me you got burned." He limped quickly across the room and gripped Alex by the shoulder. "You all right?"

"Sure." Alex pointed at the booth. "The doctor here took care of me."

"Perone, come in!" Jimbo called from behind the screen. Alex and Tito squeezed in next to the table. Jimbo finished a small leaf, then released the foot pedal. "How's that turtle holding up?"

"It's healed better than the rest of me." Tito turned his shoulder to Jimbo. The man on the table craned his head to see, and everyone admired the sea turtle.

"Designed by Alex here," Jimbo said.

"That's right," Tito said. "I copied it from the one he painted on our surfboards. *He's* the artist."

Alex felt warm with relief. It sounded as if Tito had forgiven him.

Jimbo returned to his work. The engine hummed as the needle slowly colored the heavy man's flesh. "So tell me what happened in the canyon," he said.

Tito frowned. "We lost a lot of stuff in the bus. Guess this isn't my year. But it sounds as if things would have been worse if Beekman hadn't warned the firefighters." He slapped Alex's shoulder. "So, Jimbo's put you to work? Is there any new stuff on the walls?"

"Lots," Jimbo said. "Take a look."

Tito went out. Alex listened as his uneven tread circled the room. "Nice panther," Tito called. "Hey, Alex, this one of yours?"

"Yeah. You like it?"

"A lot." Tito slipped back in behind the screen. "When I'm flush again, maybe I'll put it on my other shoulder."

"Better save your money for a place to live." Jimbo took the paper palette from Alex and set it on the counter. "You're done, Beekman," he said. "It's past eight. You guys go out on the town. Joe here would probably like me to quit shooting the breeze with you and finish up. Right?"

The pudgy man groaned. "Anything to get it over with. I forgot how much this hurts."

"Hurts like hell, but you live through it," Alex and Tito said in unison.

Jimbo groaned. "Either you know each other too well—or else I say that too often. Get out of here." He waved them off.

Outside, Alex felt awkward. "Where should we go?"

"Let's walk on the beach," Tito said. "It's low tide."

They followed the ramp down to the ocean. It was still light, but shadows were spreading across the sand, and the beach was nearly deserted. They took off their shoes and hid them under a cardboard box. Alex glanced at his friend, clearing his throat. The conversation was up to him. "Sorry about the way I acted yesterday," he said. "I don't know why I freaked out."

Tito raised an eyebrow, but said nothing. They reached the hard-packed sand near the surf and walked north at the edge of the water, the foam coiling up around their feet. Alex had to slow his long stride so Tito could keep up.

A big wave smashed unexpectedly nearby, boiling around their knees like soap and spraying them from head to foot. Tito stumbled; Alex grabbed him and danced to the side, almost collapsing under his weight. Slowly, gently, they regained their balance together, but didn't let go. Alex turned and wrapped his arms around Tito's back, resting his cheek on his friend's soft hair. Even though Tito was so much shorter, Alex felt like a child who'd found his way home. He began to cry.

"Easy, man." Tito led him gently up the beach and sat him down in the soft sand, keeping an arm draped over his shoulder. Alex wept until he felt scoured out, then untucked his shirt, wiped his face on the tail, and fell back in the sand, shuddering. A solitary planet gleamed just above the horizon, where the sun had disappeared. The surf hissed and withdrew, slowly and steadily. The world goes on, Alex thought. His life was turned inside out, but the planet kept pulsing, its heartbeat steady even while his own escalated to fever pitch.

He closed his eyes, and when he opened them, Tito leaned over, his eyes sad and dark, and kissed Alex gently on the lips. Alex groaned softly when Tito pulled away. It was over too fast! He wanted to grab his friend around the neck, to pull him close and kiss him again, but he didn't dare. His heart would break.

Tito sat back and twitched his hair off his shoulders, his eyes scanning Alex's face. "You risked your life for me," he said. "I can't get over it."

"What else would I do?" Alex asked. "You're my best friend."

Tito took Alex's hand, tracing his palm gently with his index finger. "I was right, wasn't I?" he said at last.

Alex hesitated before he answered. He forced himself to shut out his heart, hammering in his throat, to narrow his focus to a single point, as if he were dribbling a ball down the soccer field and suddenly saw a narrow gap, a hole in the defense with empty air, green grass, and an unprotected goal box beckoning beyond. In those moments, he would shoot with his whole being, aim for the goal as if his life depended on it, his eyes following the ball's curved trajectory. Once the kick was launched, it was out of his control. He could only pray the ball would find its sweet home in the far corner of the net. There was no way to do it over, to make it right a second time. And once he'd spoken the words he needed to say now, his life would never be the same again.

He sat up so his eyes were level with the friend who'd once dazzled him by dancing on a school lunch tray in an open courtyard, the friend who'd dared him to take every other risk in his life—including this one, the hardest yet.

When the words finally came, they poured easily, like smooth oil. "Yeah, you were right, Tito. I'm gay. Just like you."

Tito clasped him in a bear hug. They held each other close for a long time, until someone passing by hissed, "Dirty faggots," and spit at them, just missing Tito's shoulder.

They jumped back, scrambled to their feet, and hurried up the beach into the shadows of the palisades, Tito dragging his leg at a fast limp. When they sat down again, Alex felt the world spin, as it had the only time he'd ever been drunk. He dug his hands deep into the sand for support.

"Jesus, Tito," Alex said. "All this time, I've been trying to deny it, pretending to be someone else—it's exhausting. I've been asleep my whole life, especially the last six years."

Tito sank into the soft sand beside him, his bad leg stretched out at an angle. "Six years? What happened then?" he asked.

Alex smiled. "Sixth grade, idiot. Las Cruces School playground. The day we met. It was like the movies: love at first sight. Only I knew something was wrong. You weren't supposed to feel that way about a guy."

Tito laughed. "I remember. I talked to some kid afterward and he said, 'Who's the beautiful blond?' Took me a full minute to realize he meant Rita, not you."

Alex lay back in the sand. His head still whirled. "My poor sister. She's not going to know how to deal with any of this."

"Why not? Rita's cool."

Alex smiled sadly. "Yeah, you're right. She probably figured me out years ago. But not you. She'll be blown away when she hears your story."

Tito cocked his head. "Why?"

"She was in love with you, too." Alex began to laugh. Everything suddenly seemed so absurd. "Jesus! Who'd believe my sister and I were crazy about the same guy!" The few bright stars blurred with his tears. He found Tito's hand and held tight. "It's too late for you and me, isn't it?"

Tito squeezed back, then let go gently. "Afraid so. Ken and I are tight. It's true he reminds me of you. That's what drew me to him right off. Of course, he won't drop everything to try something crazy, the way you would. He digs his heels in, where I know you'd say: Go for it. But he's taken the biggest risk of all: coming out to his parents, his friends. He was so public about being gay, I knew I'd have to come out as well, to be with him. He's a few years older—goes to UCLA part time. His parents are up in Oregon. They're cool about who he is, and I thought: Hey, I can do this, too, share the truth with my family. Little did I know . . . "

"When did you tell them?"

"March."

Alex nodded, rubbing his arms. The air felt damp and soft as the last light faded. "That's when I started to worry. I was leaving you messages, Rita was writing you letters—I guess you never got them."

"No. My parents made sure of that."

"What made you tell them?"

"A lot of things. Raquel guessed, and my mom seemed suspicious. But mainly, I couldn't stand wearing a mask anymore. Luckily, Ken was there when all hell broke loose." He brushed Alex's face with his fingers, making him shudder. "I'm sorry. When I said it should have been you—I'm not sure that's right. Our friendship was all about denying it. We might have kept up the pretense a long time—until neither one of us could stand the frustration anymore."

Alex sat up and leaned gently against him. "It's always been torture for me."

Tito laughed and pulled him close. "Really? I thought I was the only one."

Alex let Tito hold him up. He was trembling again. "Did you shake all the time, when you first admitted it?"

Tito nodded. "I thought I had a weird disease. It's called fear. Try to stay cool. You'll make it."

Alex couldn't imagine how he would deal with anything from now on. Tito was right; they'd been wearing masks. Alex had kept his on for seventeen years. Now that he'd stripped it off, there was no way to put it back. He felt naked, exposed. "What do I do now?"

"Don't go too fast. You might want to keep things quiet in Vermont. Some guys who come out in high school say it's hell, depending on where you live. I never went back to school last spring. After everything else that happened, the classroom seemed irrelevant."

Alex thought about Griswold. Even though Tovitch had graduated, his cronies would still be cruising the halls. Could he put up with that crap for another year?

"Your ad said you were here for the summer," Tito said. "Did Rita come, too?"

"No—it's just me and my dad." Alex brushed sand from his hair. "I had to find you." His voice caught. "Dad's working on a TV script that could turn into a much longer series—and if that happens, he might stay on longer." Alex met Tito's gaze for a long minute. He was almost getting used to the trembling, although it made him feel as if he had a constant fever.

"So you might stick around?"

Alex closed his eyes. "I don't know. I'm pretty confused about everything right now."

"Yeah. Don't push yourself. It's weird, at first." Tito took his hands. "If you stay, you could hang out with Ken and me."

"Three's a crowd," Alex said softly. It was too painful to think about standing on the sidelines, watching Tito and Ken together. "Before I knew about Ken, I had this idea that when fall came, Dad would leave and I'd move in with you. Escape the torture of Griswold High, where I'm dead meat. When I talked to your mom and found out you weren't living at home anymore, I thought I had it made. You and I could be outcasts together. I assumed you'd take me in. I still wasn't admitting we were gay—just that we were friends, lifelong buddies. But when I saw you with Ken—that was the end of my dreams, I guess. And then, last night, I was going to pull you out of the burning bus, save you somehow—so you'd want to be with me again. What a fantasy." Alex dug his feet into the sand and scooped it over his legs to warm them. The air was getting cold. "This is embarrassing," he said.

"Go on." Tito squeezed his shoulder. "I love hearing you tell the truth."

"Yeah. It feels good to me, too." Alex took another deep breath. "When I was biking into Topanga, I wished something would happen to Ken. It was horrible, to feel that jealous. But I somehow thought, if he was gone, we could have things back the way they were. Your leg would heal, and we'd go surfing together, get ready for our year in Hawaii—" Alex caught himself, hearing what he was saying. "Jesus, Tito. All I've thought about is myself. What about your leg? *Will* you surf again? Can you play soccer?"

"Surfing, sure. If I have anything to say about it. Maybe not Oahu's Pipeline, but Point Zero, no problem. I don't know about soccer—it doesn't seem as important now." Tito pushed his hair back over his shoulders. "The big issue for me is just surviving."

"Where will you go?"

"We're staying with a friend of Ken's. I guess we'll find another place, or try to salvage the bus. We can still rent the land—although it's pretty gruesome up there, with everything burned to a crisp. Ken's the one who persuaded me to take the GEDs. I'm going to community college in the fall if I can get some loans together." He sifted sand through his fingers. "Funny—that's one advantage to being eighteen and having your parents kick you out—you look great on financial aid forms."

Alex shivered and stood up. Tito had new dreams now, but his own were disappearing, like water vapor skimming off the top of a triple overhead. "How do you get around, anyway? I didn't see a car up there."

"You're right. We don't own one." Tito smiled and held out his hand for a hoist up. They stood side-by-side without touching, so close Alex could smell the familiar sweet and sour scent of Tito's sweat. "Remember, I was saving for a cycle? That part of my life actually worked out. I bought an old Yamaha. It's a beauty. Come on, check it out."

They rode the Yamaha up into Topanga to look for Alex's bike, scooting past the police barrier when Tito showed his resident pass. Alex strapped Ken's helmet under his chin and gripped Tito around the waist, tucking his chin against the leather jacket Tito had pulled from his pouch. It was just like his dream, but sad. He'd found Tito, only to lose him, all in a matter of days. Alex let the tears fall again as they booked it up the PCH, the engine wailing. By the time they reached the canyon turn, Alex had stopped crying. His soul hurtled ahead into the darkness, somewhere just beyond the sweep of the Yamaha's headlamp. In spite of his sorrow, he felt more alive than he'd ever been, his vision clear and dry as bone.

They found the bike where Alex had left it: locked to the tree and unharmed. The firebreak was a few hundred yards above them, and the live oak was untouched. Alex grinned. "At least *something* worked out."

Tito gripped Alex by the shoulder. "You've got everything ahead of you, man. This is the hardest time, believe me. Once you admit it to yourself—the rest is painful, but you live through it."

Alex smiled. Jimbo's words applied to life as well as needles.

"I'll come back for the bike when they reopen the canyon," Alex said. "No one will take it tonight." They rode in silence to Venice, with Alex savoring each moment that his arms encircled his friend.

The little house was lit from one end to the other, which surprised him; usually his father was compulsive about switching the lights off. Tito held the Yamaha steady with his feet outstretched while Alex climbed off and unsnapped the helmet. "Want to come in?"

"I'd better not. We don't know if your dad is a safe bet or not. And you need some time to figure out your next moves. Remember, five miles an hour, not cruising speed."

"Right." Alex stood looking into Tito's eyes, lit by the street-light. "How can I reach you?"

"I'll call you at the shop tomorrow. We'll stay in touch. I want you to get to know Ken—if you can stand it. Believe me, you're going to need someone to talk to. And we'll be there."

Alex wasn't ready for Ken yet, but he didn't say so. "Thanks for listening tonight." He put out his hand and they shook solemnly, as they had the first time they met. Then Tito pulled him close, into a rough and fast embrace, his helmet knocking Alex's cheek.

"Good luck, man. You're stronger than you think."

Alex watched him peel off down the street, taking the corner in a sweet, slanting curve. His heart felt as if it had broken and mended, all within the course of a few hours.

He turned to look at his house and his breath stopped. Rita stepped into the open kitchen door, her body backlit, her long hair blowing in front of her face. She stepped aside and Klema joined her, his face split wide by a grin.

The shakes came down over Alex again, as strong and penetrating as the Santa Anas. "Twin ESP," he whispered to himself. "Just when I need her the most. Unbelievable." He strode up the walk to the house, grabbed his sister around the waist, and twirled her in a circle until she screeched at him to stop.

eighteen

Alex hugged his sister tight, pounded Klema on the back, then held Rita again. She gasped and exclaimed over his singed hair and eyebrows, and then said, "Was that Tito, on the motorcycle? Why didn't he come in?" Before Alex could answer, she and Klema began talking at once, pelting him with questions until Alex gripped his ears and cried, "Hold it! Hold it!" They stopped, laughing, and Alex demanded, "What the *hell* are you guys doing here?"

Rita's eyes darkened from navy to cobalt, a sure sign she'd turned serious. "You were screaming for help," she told him. "I heard you. I woke up from a sound sleep, standing next to my bed with my face feeling scorched, even though it was a cool night."

She threw Klema a shy glance, and it didn't take twin intuition for Alex to see that she and Klema were definitely a pair. So Klema had worked fast.

"I called Dave," Rita went on, "woke him up. He told me about the fires; he'd seen it on the news. I called Dad, and found out you really *had* been in the fire, so I wasn't totally wacko. Next thing I know, Dave's all wound up about these U.S. Air student hops, and before long, we're making reservations, at four in the morning—"

Dave? Alex grinned. Klema had really gone over the edge, if he was letting her call him that. He listened while she rattled on, explaining how Klema's mother had become excited about the plan, driven them to Burlington for the early flight out; how they hadn't slept all night. Alex watched Klema, and realized, with relief, that he would never look at a girl with the goofy, shit-eating grin that was plastered across Klema's face right now. Thank God. No more faking. He held on to the counter.

"Are you listening?" Rita asked. "I said, is there anything to eat in this house?"

"Not much," Alex said, but they set about fixing a snack as if they'd only been apart five minutes: Alex toasting and buttering bagels, Klema finding glasses and scrounging for ice, Rita cutting up cantaloupe and getting excited about the fresh orange juice in the fridge ("I knew there was *something* I missed about L.A."), all of them laughing as they loaded a tray and carried it into the living room where Alex realized, for the first time, that Chris wasn't around.

"Where's Dad?" he asked.

"There's a note in the kitchen, saying he'll be at the studio until late. Which is good—we can talk."

"Does he know you're coming?"

"Nope. The mothers kept it quiet."

"How'd you get into the house?"

Rita laughed. "You know Dad. He's so predictable—the key is always under a flowerpot."

She sat on the couch beside Alex, leaning against him. Klema settled into the soft armchair nearby, rubbing her leg with his bare foot. Alex shook his head. What a day! Admitting the truth to Tito, then coming home to find his sister and Klema were an item, as Klema would say—it was too much to take in all at once.

They ate their snack quickly, talking in snatches. Rita's laughter came bubbling out in unexpected places. Her eyes danced and sparkled. Alex had never seen her so happy. "Looks like you two are having a good time," he said.

Klema's freckles darkened. "No kidding," he said, his voice suddenly gone shy. "So tell us, Beekman—what was going on? Was Tito in the fire?"

The room was still, allowing other sounds to filter in. Palm fronds scratched softly against the open jalousie windows. The big fan above them sliced through the warm air. The sound of traffic wafted toward them in layers: the close hiss of Ocean Avenue, the distant rumble of the freeway.

"It's a long story," Alex said at last.

Klema drained his juice and settled back in his chair, his legs sprawled, his hands locked behind his head. "Why do you think we came?" he said. "Let's hear it."

Alex took a deep breath and began at the beginning, from surfing with Hawk to finding Raquel to the clues at Jimbo's that led him up into Topanga. He watched his sister closely as he described the bus on Weasel Creek Road, the shock of seeing Tito's face with its angry scar, his terrible limp. She cringed, but listened quietly as he went on to last night, and the sirens wailing on the Pacific Coast Highway. "I went bananas," Alex said. "One minute, I was fine, and the next second, I decided Tito was trapped inside his bus and I had to get him out. I was a maniac." He found his sister's eyes. "I thought it was an ESP thing, and if I didn't pay attention to my hunch, he'd die. But of course, I was wrong. He was at work in the Palisades, selling surfboards, while I was killing myself, getting chased by the fire. What an idiot."

"Thank God you made it." Rita leaned against him. "I still haven't learned to tell the difference between fear and psychic intuition. I had the same feelings last night—I was all worked up, and then thought maybe I was just inventing it." She waited, and when Alex didn't say anything else, she said, "You've left out the most important part. Why did Tito's parents kick him out? How did he get hurt?"

Alex glanced at Klema. His hazel eyes flickered, but gave nothing away. So he *is* a guy you can trust, Alex thought. He liked that.

"Tito's gay," Alex said quietly. "He lives in the canyon with

Ken, his—his lover." God, it hurt to use that word, but he kept going. "Ken took him in after his father beat him up."

Rita's face was ashen. She leaned her head back against the couch. "Wait a minute. Mr. Perone beat up his kid—because he's gay? Is he sick?"

"Mr. Perone thinks *Tito* is sick," Alex said, "so Tito has to keep a low profile. He's afraid his father might come after him again."

Rita put her hand on Alex's knee. She was quiet for a long time. "Oh, my God," she said at last. "This is so bizarre. But it explains everything."

"It does?" Alex felt flushed and confused. Inside his head, he heard Tito saying, *Go slow,* but he realized he couldn't do that, not with his sister—she was always one step ahead.

"Of course." Rita sat up straight, looked at Klema, and blushed. "This is embarrassing. Dave, don't hate me."

Klema grinned. "Not a chance."

Rita turned back to Alex. "I used to have such a crush on Tito—and—" she gasped, nearly choking with embarrassment. "This will sound so stuck up, but I have to say it. I could never stand the way he just *ignored* me, as if I didn't even exist. I mean, he was always nice to me, and treated me like a friend, but he just didn't care that I was a girl. Know what I mean?" She studied Alex, realization flooding her face. "He was really crazy about *you.* Wasn't he?"

"That's right." He *was,* Alex thought. He gripped the arm of the couch and swore silently to himself. Just last night he was still able to put up a wall when anyone got too close. Now, the barriers had disappeared. He felt as if he were Tito's turtle, without his shell. He lay naked and vulnerable, his soft body open to the sun and wind.

Rita held his hand tight. Her eyes brimmed. "He only cared about you. And that's why—" she glanced at Klema.

"Go on," Alex said softly. "It's okay if he hears." His

antennae were finally working, and he knew what his sister would say before the words came out.

"That's why you were so upset when he disappeared," she said. "Because—" She gulped, unable to finish the sentence.

Alex had to help her. "Because I'm gay, too."

Rita nodded and buried her head against his chest. Alex stroked her hair to keep his hands from shaking. He looked at Klema over the top of her head. Klema's face was as frozen as his hands, which clutched the arms of the chair. He heard Tito again, warning him to take his time. Had he made a mistake, telling Klema? Too late now. "Are you surprised?" Alex asked him.

"Yes and no." Klema leaned forward. The gold flecks in his eyes made him seem more intense. "I had a hunch, that afternoon at the bagel place—but I wasn't sure." To Alex's amazement, he extended his hand awkwardly. "Congratulations," he said.

Alex stared, puzzled, as they shook. "For what?"

Klema sat back, his face red. "Hell, I don't know. For being brave. Telling the truth. You know, all the hard stuff." He looked supremely uncomfortable, and Alex turned to his sister for reassurance, but she jumped up and ran for the bathroom. Alex felt queasy himself. What the hell. If Rita couldn't deal with this, who could?

Alex and Klema listened to her sob, then to the sound of the water running hard. Klema half stood, then dropped back in his chair. "She'll be okay," he said, but he didn't seem convinced. "So, how do you feel?" he asked.

"I don't know." Alex's legs bounced, and he didn't even try to keep them still. Maybe he'd always be this nervous; maybe it was part of his new life: feeling antsy and afraid all the time. "Wired. Excited. Scared. Relieved. It's not something you can undo. Once you're out, the closet door shuts behind you."

"What are you going to say to Mom and Dad?" Rita stood in the doorway, blowing her nose.

"I don't know." Alex tried to smile. "That's my answer to every question these days." He watched her carefully, wondering if she realized how much he cared about her reaction. "Rita, why are you so sad? It's not the end of the world for me, you know." She sat down beside him again, wiping her eyes on her shirtsleeve. "Come on," Alex begged. "My ESP isn't working. Tell me what's wrong. Do you think I'm a horrible person? Why are you crying?"

"Because I should have known. You must have felt so alone—for so long. And none of us knew." Her eyes streamed.

"Rita, how could you know? I was hiding it from everyone—especially myself." They held each other tight while Klema looked from one to the other, unsure of what to do. Suddenly Rita pulled away, laughing through her tears.

"You know what? We can go cruising for guys together."

Alex winked at Klema. "I know someone who might object."

"Damned right." Klema reached for Rita's hand and pulled her onto his lap, wiping her tears with his shirttail. "Keep your eyes on me, babe." Rita nestled against him, her legs dangling over the arm of the chair.

Alex stared up at the ceiling, where the big fan swirled slowly, ticking gently through the warm air. Rita squeezed his knee. "Alex," she said softly.

He met her eyes, identical to his, and felt locked in their safety. He could read her thoughts again, clear as his own. "Yes."

"You know I love you. No matter what."

"Yeah," he said, his voice breaking. "You're the best. I know."

They were all quiet for a long time. With every breath, Alex realized, he was moving forward into his new life. He tasted terror in his throat, like the fear that chased him with the fire the night before, but it came with a new sensation, something he couldn't name yet.

"I was worried when you left," Rita said suddenly. "I thought you might never come back."

"That was my plan. I thought I could live with Tito. Little did I know." He tried to smile, to cover the pain, but Rita saw through it, of course.

"It must have hurt, to find him with some other guy."

Alex closed his eyes. Hurt wasn't the word. Agony was more like it. Right in the chest, too. A broken heart, he was discovering, was a real sensation in the body, not just an idea.

A car door slammed on the street. Alex stood up, wanting to bolt, to run on the beach, anything to release the tension. But it was too late; his father's footsteps scuffed up the concrete walk.

Rita jumped from Klema's lap. "It's Dad!" she whispered. Klema and Alex got up and stood awkwardly beside her. The kitchen door squeaked open and shut.

"Alex? You here?" Chris called.

"Hey, Dad. In the living room."

Alex hesitated in the middle of the shag rug, unsure what to do next. He had the absurd urge to hide behind the curtains, but of course he didn't, just stood there feeling foolish while his father came in, grumbling about all the lights being on. "You having a party or something? The place looks like a ship—" His jaw dropped as he caught sight of Rita, then Klema. "Wha—"

"Surprise!" Rita threw her arms around her father. Chris sputtered, dropped his box of diskettes, and staggered backward, nearly falling over. "Rita, what on earth—"

He gaped at Klema, who was shifting from one foot to the other, looking embarrassed. Alex rescued him. "Dad, remember our friend David Klema, from Griswold?"

"Of course, of course." Chris dumped the rest of his things on the couch, took off his glasses, and rubbed his eyes, as if he didn't trust what he was seeing. "Excuse me for seeming stupid—but did I miss something?"

Rita burst out laughing and grabbed her father's hands. "That's the point, Dad! We wanted to surprise you." She explained about it being fourth of July weekend, that there were these cheap fares, that Klema had never seen L.A. "And I was worried about Alex," she said.

"Yes. Aren't we all."

The weight of his father's words made Alex's shoulders sag. Chris sank onto the couch, pulled off his shoes, and rested his feet on the table. Alex studied his father's puffy face, the deep pouches under his eyes, and felt guilty. But suddenly he realized something. Like Rita, like Klema, like his mother—who didn't know yet what was about to hit her—his father had grown up knowing who he was, while Alex had been split between two people all his life—the boy he'd shown to the outside world, and the one he'd kept hidden behind the mask. Now he could begin to be whole. But only if he told the truth.

"You can stop worrying, Dad," Alex said.

"Really? How convenient. Then maybe you'd like to get me a beer."

"In a minute."

Chris looked up at his son and blinked. "Why do I feel as if this whole summer is about secrets happening behind my back?"

"No more secrets," Alex said.

"Alex—" Rita warned, but he shook his head. The room was charged with electricity and he was wired into it, receiving the full blast of the current from every direction. He reached out for his sister. She slipped her cool fingers into his palm and held on tight. Alex cleared his throat. He was getting good at this.

"Dad," he said. "I have something to tell you."

nineteen

Chris Beekman's face was as white as the wall behind him. He stared vacantly into space, as if drugged. Finally he turned to Alex and said, in a choked voice, "That's the most ridiculous thing I've ever heard." He gave Klema a pointed look. "If you don't mind, I'd like to discuss this in private."

"Come with me," Rita said softly to Klema, and pulled him into Alex's room. Alex waited for the door to close before asking his father, "Why is it ridiculous?"

"Because anyone can see you're not gay," his father said.

"Oh." Alex wanted to laugh, but he didn't want to be rude. "That's because I've done such a good job of hiding it, Dad."

His father stood up suddenly, slamming his fist into his open palm. "Goddam Tito Perone! It's his fault. I never trusted that kid. He did this to you, didn't he?"

Alex struggled to keep his temper. "No one *did* anything to me, Dad. I've always known I was different. Ever since I was a kid."

His father slumped back onto the couch as if all the life were draining out of him. "Different is fine, Alex. But just because your best friend is gay doesn't mean—"

"Dad!" Alex felt his patience wearing thin. "Why do you think Tito *is* my best friend? It's because we're so alike, in every way. I've been in love with him all my life—"

"Don't talk about love that way." Chris snapped.

"Why not?" When his father didn't answer, Alex added

gently, "Dad, it's the truth. I like guys. Not girls. You even noticed that yourself."

His father groaned and held his head in his hands. "I know. If only I hadn't bugged you so much—"

Alex laughed. "But you were right. I'm not attracted to girls—not in that way. You were more perceptive than you realized."

Chris looked, his eyes pleading. "Please—at least sit down. You're so tall, it makes you seem light-years away."

Alex perched on the edge of the armchair, although he was finding it impossible to keep still. "Dad, I'm sure this feels weird. It's strange for me, too. I see why people call it coming out of the closet—because I've been hiding behind a heavy, closed door for a long time."

His father didn't seem to be listening. He struggled for words. "Alex, lots of young people have—those feelings—it's perfectly normal. When you're young. Even a phase. Some think . . . you might feel differently later on—"

The tips of his father's ears were red. This was excruciating. As far back as Alex could remember, his dad had never talked about sex to Rita or to him. In fact, it was a family joke that whenever the subject came up, Chris usually left the room. For a second, Alex wondered if Tito was right, if he should have waited to tell his parents. But if he didn't, he might keep on trembling until he shook himself to bits.

"That might be true for some people," Alex said at last. He felt as if he were explaining something to a little kid. "It's not a phase. I'm sure." Alex heard the door open behind him and felt the presence of his sister in the room again but he didn't turn around. "Tito and I need the same thing now: our parents' love. The Perones turned Tito out. I was hoping things might be different for me—but maybe not—" He breathed fast, trying to stop the tears. Rita was beside him instantly, her arm around his waist.

"Mom and Dad love you," she said softly.

But Alex kept his eyes on his father, waiting. Chris stood in the middle of the room in his stocking feet, his arms dangling. He looked old and forlorn. "Alex—I would never do that to you. Of course I love you, no matter what. It's just—"

"Just what, Dad?"

He shook his head. "I don't believe it. It's as if I woke up and discovered you'd become someone else."

Alex smiled. "You did. Only it's not the way you think. The old Alex, the one you were used to, was a lie. This one is real."

Chris took out a handkerchief, blew his nose, and went to the kitchen. He came back with a beer. "You'll have to give me time to get used to the idea."

"Sure, Dad. I'm still trying to get used to it myself." Alex stood in the middle of the room with his legs braced. It was a strange sensation, being the center of attention. For years, he realized, he'd let Rita take the lead in his family. Outside the house, he'd walked in Tito's shadow. Now he was on his own.

Rita sat on the couch. Chris perched on the arm of the chair. "What does this mean—for us?"

"For you? I guess—that you're the father of a gay son."

"What will you say to your mother?"

"The same thing I told you—but not tonight. I'm too wasted."

Chris nodded and slipped into the chair. He took a long sip of beer and put his glasses back on, sliding them up his nose. "What would you like us to tell people?'"

"Nothing," Alex said firmly. "Absolutely nothing, right now. Life in Griswold was hell. I'm not ready to broadcast it all over Vermont. The high school was enough of a nightmare last year."

Chris raised his eyebrows. He looked excited. "Then we'll forget Vermont and move back here! I'll talk to Dale. Once she knows, she'll see it's best for you. I told you, the show may expand, the producer is talking about four more episodes—"

"No way, Dad." Alex put up his hand. "Don't load all your stuff with Mom onto me. Besides, I was miserable here, too. Rita reminded me of that before we drove out, but I'd conveniently forgotten." He looked at his sister. Her face was red and blotchy, but her smile, as always, was warm and enclosing, like a hug.

The phone shrilled. Rita scooped it up, listened, and smiled. "Hi, there. Yes, I know it's Tito." Chris Beekman scowled, and Alex looked away, watching the light in his sister's face. "Just a little while ago," Rita was saying. "Our friend Dave and I decided to surprise him." She glanced at Alex. "He's right here—and he's fine. Better than I've ever seen him. Want to talk?"

Alex took the phone. He felt as if he'd just shot into the tube of an enormous, double overhead wave and was absorbing its power into his body as he rode its sleek and shining interior wall. He carried the phone into his room and fell back on his bed. Tito sounded breathless. "Man, what's going on? Your whole family showed up?"

"Just Rita—and my friend, Klema, from Griswold. I told them—told my dad—the truth."

Tito whistled. "Thought you were going to take it slow."

Alex propped himself on his elbow so he could see his father, Rita, and Klema through the doorway. Rita was choosing music from his stack of CDs. "I guess I don't understand about slow," Alex said.

Tito laughed. "No. I noticed that the first time I tried to take you on the soccer field."

"Jesus," Alex said. "I'm shaking again. So what's up? Why did you call?"

"To see if you were all right," Tito said. "The night I admitted the truth to myself, I was shook, even though Ken was with me. It was months before I dared tell my family.

You're so fast, you're in overdrive. How's your dad taking it—
or can you say?"

"All right, considering. We'll talk tomorrow." The music
began in the next room, the Spin Doctors singing "What Time
Is It?" Alex swayed and drummed his fingers on the blanket,
itching to dance. "When do you go to work in the morning?"

"Not until noon," Tito said.

"Great. How about coming with me to Point Zero—I
want to teach Klema to surf. I'll pick you up early."

Tito hesitated, then said, "All right. Will I like the guy?"

Alex laughed. "Guaranteed." He lowered his voice. "He's
Rita's boyfriend."

"Lucky dude."

Alex arranged to meet Tito at Raquel's beach club at
seven-thirty. When he said good-bye, the Spin Doctors were
wailing. His father sat on the couch, tapping his feet absently,
looking like something dug out of the lost and found. Klema
and Rita pushed back the furniture. Alex rolled up the rug and
the three of them danced, gyrating and pounding the floor.
The music settled in his belly, rang in his head, buzzed down
his arms and legs. He was alive, yet full of terror. In every cell.
From his singed eyebrows all the way to his callused feet.

Alex was up by five the next morning. He put on Tito's
purple T-shirt, rummaged under his bed for the big sketch
pad, and slipped out without waking Klema. Rita stirred on
the couch as he tiptoed past, but didn't open her eyes. Alex sat
at the kitchen table, drawing, for over an hour, discarding one
sketch after another until he was satisfied. He put the drawing
in a large, flat envelope and stowed it in his pack along with
drinks, bags of chips, and a big hunk of cheese. As he threw
towels into the back of the car, he noticed the thin white band
of untanned skin on his ring finger. He opened the glove box,
dug under the maps until he found the ring, and slid it back

onto his hand. The silver winked in the sun. Alex smiled. It was going to be a good day.

He forced Klema and his sister into the car at seven, ignoring Rita's complaints. Klema sat in the back, yawning widely but looking cheerful, while Rita was openly crabby. "Why are *you* so chipper this morning?" she demanded as Alex stowed his board and wet suit in the car.

He didn't answer. He couldn't explain the way he felt, even to himself. He remembered being outside in a solar eclipse, standing under a tree in downtown Griswold. While everyone else watched the sun through welder's glass, he had stared at the ground, amazed to see the veins of leaves etched on the sidewalk like intricate brocaded fabric. The passing landscape possessed that same crisp clarity now, as if he could see each molecule in the plumes of whitecaps cresting out on the dark surface of the Pacific. Every mole on his sister's cheek, each palm leaf in the swaying fronds overhead had been brought into sharp focus by a new lens inside his own eye.

He drove slowly up Ocean Avenue, pointing out landmarks to Klema, stopped to buy coffee for Rita and muffins for them all at the bakery, and continued north. How long would these sensations last? Maybe this was why some guys dropped acid? Too bad they didn't realize you could get stoned without help. Alex laughed out loud and Rita shook her head. "You're weird today," she muttered. He could only agree.

By the time they passed the Bay Street Beach parking lot, Alex was driving too fast; he had to brake suddenly to catch the entrance.

"Hey!" Rita yelled. "Watch it!" She grabbed her cup from the dash, but it sloshed hot coffee on her knees. She pulled a napkin from the paper bag, swabbing her legs. "Do you have to drive like a maniac?"

"Sorry." Alex parked near the beach. "Stay here," he said,

jumping out. "I'll be right back." He jogged across the sand to the edge of the small playground, looking behind the benches, in the shadows in back of the Dumpster, and finally, when he bent to search under the small rest room building, holding his breath against the stench of pee, he found what he was looking for: Tito's Eberly, half buried in the sand. He pulled it out, feeling a little guilty about taking the board from a kid. But it's not his, Alex reminded himself. Besides, hadn't he and Hawk both warned the punk that if Tito wanted the board back, they'd return it to him?

He stowed it on the roof next to his own, stretching the bungee cords to hold them both tight. Klema climbed out to help. "Whose board?"

"Tito's old one. Some kid picked it up—I'm stealing it back, temporarily."

Klema's head was just visible over the roof of the car. "Don't get your hopes up—I may not be able to stay on this thing."

"No one can, at first. Don't sweat it."

As Klema tightened the strap at the front, he noticed the turtle emblem. "Nice," he said. "It's like yours."

"Yeah. Turtles were our thing, back then. Perone has one on his back, now. Permanently."

"A tattoo?"

"Yeah."

"Don't think I could do that," Klema said. "It sounds too painful."

When Alex got back into the car, Rita insisted on climbing in back. "So you guys can talk. And I can sleep," she said.

But they reached the beach club before she could doze off, and when Rita saw Tito sitting on the front steps, a wet suit draped in his lap, she was suddenly wide awake. "Oh, my God," she whispered. "His face . . ."

Alex glanced at his twin in the rearview mirror, then at

Klema. Rita was obviously upset, and Klema looked nervous as hell. This could be dicey.

Alex jumped out, silently blessing Tito for not bringing Ken, and hugged his friend tight. Waves of sadness overwhelmed him again. He pulled back quickly, unable to speak. Losing Tito was nothing compared to giving him up.

Before either one of them could say anything, Rita threw her arms around Tito. "I'm so happy to see you!" She traced the scar on his cheek with her index finger. "I can't believe your dad did this."

Tito's dark eyebrows drew together. "Neither could I. But I'm still alive." He gave them a tight smile. No one knew what to say for a minute, and then Alex noticed Klema, hanging back awkwardly, his hand holding on to the car door as if he'd like to bolt. Alex pulled him forward, and as he introduced them, he wondered how he could ever have thought Klema and Tito looked alike. It must have been the square build. Otherwise, they were completely different. Klema's hazel eyes were curious, full of light, where Tito's whole face brooded. And Klema was laid-back, easygoing, while Tito's body prickled with energy and tension. They sized each other up, and Alex realized he might also be wrong about them being friends. How could he expect Klema to like the guy his girlfriend once had a crush on? Man, Alex told himself. You are still clueless about some things.

Tito squeezed Alex's shoulder. "Nice shirt."

Alex started to peel it off, but Tito stopped him. "Keep it," he said. "A memento from the fire." He tugged at the tail. "It's pretty short on you. You'll have to shrink to fit into it." He opened the back door, but Alex took his elbow and pointed toward the boards.

"Hold it, Perone," he said. "Check this out."

"My board." Tito stood on tiptoe and ran his hand over the Eberly, grinning. "Where the hell did you find this thing?"

"Bay Street. Some kid was using it. Claimed you'd abandoned it."

"I did." Tito climbed into the front seat next to Alex and strapped on his seat belt. "After Dad broke my leg, I assumed I'd never surf again. I went out on the pier in my wheelchair one night and tossed the board in. People thought I was kind of nuts—a little crowd gathered to watch. Luckily, Jimbo came out and told people to leave me alone."

Tito was quiet a minute while they pulled out across the double lanes of traffic. Alex smiled. He could just imagine Jimbo stalking through the crowd, thrusting his bearded chin into people's faces until they moved off. Alex glanced in the mirror. Klema sat with his arm draped casually over Rita's shoulder. She leaned forward a little, listening hard as Tito talked.

"There was a strong south blowing," Tito went on. "I thought for sure the board would end up in Santa Barbara." He shook his head. "Bay Street. Pathetic." He laughed, and Alex felt his friend's dark eyes on him. "I never did have much of an arm, did I?"

"That's not what I heard." Klema sat forward. "From what Alex tells me, you're good at every sport you ever tried."

Tito shrugged, but he looked pleased. He glanced at Klema. "Looks like you and I are close to the same size—a good head shorter than the tall guy here. You can wear my wet suit—the Pacific is cold, even in the summer. The board's about the right size for you, too."

"Thanks," Klema said. "I'll be lucky if I can stick to the board lying down."

"It's not that hard," Tito said. "Once you get the hang of it."

The PCH was crowded with commuters coming toward them, but traffic was spotty heading north. Alex pointed out the sights as the station wagon hugged the narrow ribbon between the coastline and the mountains: the surf shop where he'd bought his first board, the turn to Will Rogers State Park, where he'd played soccer, and the entrance to Topanga, still blocked by police barriers and a sign warning it was open to residents only. "Wonder if they'll ever let me in to pick up my bike. That's where I got stopped the other night," Alex said.

Tito shook his head. "I still can't believe you did that." He turned to grin at Rita. "Did you know your brother is crazy?"

"Yeah," she said. "I did."

Alex laughed and pressed the accelerator to the floor as a light turned green. "Hold on, everyone," he said. "Point Zero, next stop."

twenty

Six or seven guys floated beyond the breaking surf, resting on the swells like a flock of gulls. The waves broke into fine, sleek lefts. Alex stepped from the Chevy and stretched, trying to calm his nerves. He watched as one surfer rose onto a short board, crouched low and began a dance with a wave, skimming up to its lip and back down the side in a series of curving swoops and dives. Alex tried to psyche himself up, but his mouth felt dry, even though the surf was perfect—surfing lefts meant he could ride with his left foot back, the way he liked it, and the swells were steady and clean. But it was weird, teaching someone else to surf with Tito watching—the guy who taught *him* everything he knew about waves and current, wind and balance.

Tito helped him untie the boards. "Nice waves," he said, his eyes full of longing.

Alex felt like an idiot. He hadn't even thought about the way this would make Tito feel. "I'm sorry, Perone—maybe it was shitty to invite you."

Tito shrugged. "I could have said no. I wanted to see you guys."

A red Ford pickup pulled into the parking lot, its tailgate rattling, and Alex recognized the surfer who'd rescued him in Topanga on Friday night. He went over to say hello.

"Hey, it's the biker dude!" the surfer exclaimed, hopping out. "What'd you do, toast your face?"

"Afraid so," Alex said. "You survived the fire all right?"

He nodded. "We lost a shed full of garden stuff, but we

saved the house. Stayed there all night, hosing it down."

They smiled at each other. "I'm not sure I ever got your name," Alex said.

"Call me Sly. My parents had the bad taste to name me Sylvester."

"I'm Alex. This is my twin sister, Rita, and my friends, Klema and Tito."

Sly gave Rita an unabashed stare, then lifted a hand to Tito. "Perone. King of the tubular wave. Where you been? Haven't seen you in months."

"Broke my leg," Tito said.

"Massive bummer." Sly started to pull a short triple fin board from his truck, then turned back to Alex. "Don't tell me Perone's the one you were trying to rescue the other night?"

Alex grinned, embarrassed. "Yeah—and he wasn't even there. Pretty stupid, I guess."

"No *way*, dude. I'm impressed. Not sure I'd do that for anyone. You got yourself a loyal friend, Perone."

Tito nodded. "The best," he said, and for a second, Alex thought Tito was about to cry. Luckily, Sly was clueless; he just kept on talking.

"See you've got Perone's stick," he said to Klema, who was holding Tito's Eberly at an awkward angle. "You surf, man?"

"Not yet," Klema said. "They promised to teach me—and not to laugh."

"No sweat, dude," Sly said. "We were all chalk people once. I'll introduce you. The locals are fine, if you play by the rules."

He twisted his long, curly hair into a ponytail and strolled toward the water, holding his board lightly under his arm like a loaf of bread, his wet suit draped over one shoulder. Sly walked as if he expected everyone on the beach to watch him, and Alex obliged by checking the guy out from behind. Sly's back was a rack of muscles, his legs long and lean. Alex turned to find Tito's eyes on him. Perone was finally smiling. "Nice, huh," Tito said.

"You *guys*. You're embarrassing me!" Rita teased.

"So sorry." But Alex wasn't sorry at all, and he laughed out loud. So this was what it was like! Sly was straight, no doubt about that—but to admire the guy's body with Tito, out in the open—incredible.

Klema poked Alex, startling him. "*Chalk* people?"

"Surf lingo," Alex explained. "It's what we call a non-surfer."

"I can't win," Klema said. "In Vermont I'm a flatlander, in L.A. I'm a *chalk* person? Give me a break." Klema watched Sly pull on his suit and launch his board into the water. He paddled through a channel in the waves. "I didn't know guys actually talked that way, except on TV."

"Sly's really into the language, but he's good on the board, too," Tito said.

Alex struggled into his wet suit, reddening when Tito commented on how revealing it was, then showed Klema how to put grip on the front of his board, wax on the back.

Klema held up a small jar. "*Sex* wax? Come on, Beekman! What the hell does this stuff do? Or shouldn't I ask?"

Alex laughed. "Not what it says. Keeps your feet from sliding off."

"Okay," Klema said, grinning. "Guess I'll need that, won't I?"

Alex bent to snap on his leash, and Tito squeezed his shoulder through the wet suit. "Ride a few for me." Before Alex could answer, Tito had turned away, beckoning to Rita to walk with him down the beach. Alex glanced at Klema. "Ready?"

"Guess so. Look, if I drown, tell my mom I had a good life, will you?"

Alex smiled. "You'll survive. You might swallow some of

the Pacific, though. Luckily it's not as polluted out here as in Santa Monica."

They carried their boards into the water, and Alex taught Klema how to launch himself into a channel created by the retreating current, and then, once they were out, gave him pointers on getting to his feet, on the instant to rise up and find the wave's inner power. "Just try to stand up," Alex said. "Pretend you're snowboarding on moving moguls."

For an hour or more, Klema spent more time under the board, or tumbling headfirst into boiling foam, than on the Eberly. But finally, he caught one wave, standing for a full half minute before losing it. When he came up beaming, Alex could see he was hooked.

Alex left him on his own and launched himself into the first wave of a double set. He caught it perfectly, and was even able to walk the board, then turn and speed ahead of the breaking lip, keeping his board just inches from the curling curtain of gray water pulling closed behind him. He felt exhilarated, and when he mounted the wave at the last instant, throwing himself into a lipper over the top into the trough behind, he stifled a shout. A perfect ride. Flat on his belly, his heart pounding against his suit, his arms pulling him over the oncoming swells, he glanced toward shore.

Damn! Tito and Rita sat way down the beach, their heads close together, lost in talk. He'd caught the perfect wave—and no one noticed? Alex felt hurt, like a little kid. He stopped paddling a minute, catching his breath. Why should he care if they were watching? Who was he doing this for, anyway? As he paddled over the next set of swells, he realized he'd often surfed for Tito, not himself. He'd been that way on Rollerblades, too—not to mention the soccer field. Last fall, he'd touched Tito's ring every time he'd made a goal, giving him credit. What the hell. Tito hadn't scored the goals. *He* had.

Alex felt nervous. It had been so much easier, letting Tito's long shadow fall across his face, hiding who he was. Now all that was changed. He was out in the sun, on his own.

He paddled north, his eyes on the rocky shoreline rather than the swells. If Klema hadn't waved and pointed out to sea, just then, he might have given up, headed for shore, but instead he joined his friend, fighting the empty feeling that came from someplace strange and unexplained.

"Look at that train coming in!" Klema yelled.

Alex smiled. Klema was catching on to the lingo. He sat up on his board. A big set was cresting and re-forming, as though some deep sea creature were underneath the waves, pushing them higher with its forehead. "Nice," Alex called. "Move fast, or you'll miss it."

Klema paddled furiously, but he stood up too soon and lost it; his board shot out from under him and he disappeared, the Eberly jumping and writhing as if alive. Alex paddled over the lip of the wave just before it crashed into a boil just beyond him. He sat up straight, waiting for Klema to surface. When he finally did, he looked like he'd been pummeled. Klema clung to his board, drifting into shore in the backwash, and when he stood up, he staggered a few steps, then bent over to retch in the sand. God, did Alex remember those days! How long had it taken him to find his balance? Days? Weeks?

Sly paddled toward him. "Got slammed on that one—but he's learning. How come I've never seen you here before?" Sly asked.

"I've been in Vermont," Alex said. "I just came back for the summer."

"Better stick around," Sly said. "Looks like you belong here."

"Thanks," Alex said, although he wasn't so sure. Right now, he felt as if he were in a plane circling an unknown airport, with no idea where he would be when he landed.

"Perone's waving at you," Sly said.

Alex turned. Tito was pointing to his watch. "Damn. Guess we have to leave."

"Bummer. You guys got some real-life stuff to do?"

"Afraid so. Jobs. Back to reality."

Sly laughed. "*This* is reality, dude. The rest is all a bad dream. But hey, come back. You're always welcome." Before Alex could answer, Sly was off, paddling toward the next set.

Alex watched him go, and glanced along the line at the other surfers, each in his own world, each waiting on a lonely watch for the perfect wave, and knew why he felt empty. He missed the sense of sport as a team, the constant back and forth between players who were always connected by the ball. Surfers rarely spoke; Sly was breaking the code by coming close enough to say a few words. Without Tito to banter with, he was alone with his ecstasy.

But then Alex watched Sly rise to catch a wave. You think too much, Beekman, he told himself. What's wrong with doing something alone, if it feels this good? He paddled to meet the next train and rode the smallest of the set in toward shore, his knees bent, his arms outstretched like wings. This last one was all for himself. And that was as it should be.

It was hard to tear Klema away, even though he'd only found his legs a few times. "It would be easy to get addicted to this stuff," he said, peeling off his suit. "Especially if I ever learn to stand up." He handed the suit to Tito, who shook his head.

"Keep it," Tito said. "I can't use it now. Just leave it with Alex when you go back."

Rita kissed Klema on the mouth and rubbed his head, brushing out the sand.

"Poor thing," she said. "You got trashed." She stood talking to him while Alex and Tito carried the boards to the car.

"Enjoy that?" Tito asked.

Alex nodded. "But it's not the same without you to egg me on."

"Maybe I'll be out there by the end of the summer," Tito said. "Ken's good, too. Not as graceful as you, though." The wind whipped Tito's long hair across his face, hiding his scar, and for a moment, he looked like his old self. "Think you'll stick around this fall?" Tito asked.

Alex shrugged. "I don't know. I'm not sure where I belong yet."

Tito stood his board upright in the sand and looked out to sea. A lone freighter crawled on the horizon. "I know what you mean."

Alex met Tito's dark eyes, then glanced away. Everything felt different today. He thought of a sad song his mother used to play, where the man sang that the distance between him and his lover was "growing by inches and miles." Tito seemed farther away now than when Alex lived in Vermont. The empty feeling rose in his chest as he watched another wave train roll in.

"Look at those big mothers," Tito said. "Running all the way from Japan."

Alex started for the car, but Tito touched his elbow, so lightly Alex almost didn't notice. "See you're wearing my ring again," Tito said. He hesitated. "We'll always be friends."

It didn't sound like a question, but Alex heard the worry in his voice. "It's different than before," Alex admitted. "But I'll always love you." He swallowed the bitter taste of jealousy, the knowledge of what he'd lost. "Don't disappear again," he warned. "Finding you was hard work."

"That's because you weren't looking for me."

Alex stared into his friend's black eyes, puzzled. Before he could ask Tito what he meant, Rita and Klema came hurrying toward them, trudging through the deep sand, pushing each other playfully.

Tito turned away, and Alex followed him to the car.

* * *

They let Tito out at the beach club, where he took off on his Yamaha, and then Alex drove to the pier. "Where are we going?" Rita asked.

"To Jimbo's," Alex said. "I want to show you where I work."

He grabbed his pack and led them down the pier, walking so fast, Rita had to jog to keep up. "What's the rush?" she asked.

Alex didn't answer. He was afraid he might lose his nerve. As he expected, Jimbo was dozing outside in the shade, his arms crossed on his chest. Alex glanced at Klema and his sister. Rita's eyes widened as she took in Jimbo's tattoos. Klema pursed his lips in a silent whistle and shook his head from side to side.

Jimbo set his chair down with a thump when Alex spoke to him. "Well, Beekman. You're here early."

"Yeah," Alex said. "This is my twin sister, Rita—and my friend, Klema. They flew in from Vermont to surprise me."

Jimbo stood up, grinning, and shook hands. "Pleased to meet you. You come for tattoos?"

"No." Rita shook her head, laughing. "Alex just wants to show us around—"

"Actually," Alex said, taking a deep breath, "I *am* here for a tattoo."

"Heavy-duty!" Klema exclaimed, and Rita clutched his arm. "Alex, Dad will have a fit—"

"So what? It's my body, not his."

Jimbo nodded. "Quite right. You want a turtle, like Perone's?"

Alex shook his head. Until a few days ago, the sea turtle was the only tattoo he'd considered. Now everything had changed. "I brought my own design," he said.

Jimbo rubbed his hands together. "Wonderful. Let's see what you've got."

Alex spread the drawing flat on the counter inside the shop. "Coyote, the trickster," Jimbo said. He held it up to the light. Alex felt good about the drawing. He'd captured the coyote the way he remembered him: trotting in an easy, graceful lope, his head held high, ears pricked, amber eyes steady but cunning.

"This is a beauty," Jimbo said. "I bet we get a lot of calls for this one—if you're willing to share it with customers."

"Sure," Alex said.

Klema stood back, admiring the design. "This looks different from your other drawings."

Jimbo agreed. "It's looser, less controlled."

That fits, Alex thought.

"Aren't you afraid of the needles?" Rita asked.

"Are you kidding—after what I've done in the last few days?" Alex said, laughing. "Tattooing should be a piece of cake."

Jimbo went to the thermofax machine and transferred the coyote to a stencil, then held it up for Alex's approval. "It will take almost an hour—and you know my rates. That's a few days' work for you—"

"No problem." Alex pulled off Tito's shirt, eager to get going.

"Where do you want it?" Jimbo asked.

"On my right arm. So it looks as if he's running toward my back."

"Left-handed, aren't you? Good enough. Why don't you choose your own colors. And if you want, I can add a little background—"

"Great. I saw this one coming out of the chaparral. Maybe you can show the underbrush." Alex chose browns, blues, and greens from the line of bottles on the shelf, squeezing the colored inks into the red caps. He pointed to a silvery blue at the end of the row. "I'd like this color for the coyote," he told Jimbo. "He was almost blue—maybe it was the light."

Rita and Klema hovered at the edge of the booth, asking

questions. Alex held still while Jimbo shaved his arm clean. "Want to watch?" Jimbo asked. Rita shook her head. "No way. Not unless you want to deal with me fainting."

"Forget it," Alex said. So Rita went outside with a stack of tattoo magazines, while Klema perched on a stool nearby. Alex lay flat on his stomach and turned his head away. The needles hurt like hell at first. He gripped the edge of the table with his hands until Jimbo said, "Ease up, boy. Breathe deep, let those muscles go—it won't hurt so much."

Just what he always told his customers. And he was right. When Alex made a conscious effort to release the tension, the pain wasn't so intense, although he couldn't help feeling as if a sewing machine were running down his arm. The buzz of the needle was as annoying as a dentist's drill.

"The coyote is crafty," Jimbo said after a while. "Lots of Native American tales feature coyote the trickster."

Alex nodded. But that wasn't why he'd picked a coyote for his first— and maybe only—tattoo. It was the way the animal had appeared out of nowhere, the way it looked into and through him—eyes intelligent, movements rangy and free, a creature completely unconcerned with what anyone might think of it—and then, while he was watching, it disappeared; melted away. A phantom, shaman, magician. The trick Alex had always wanted to pull himself.

twenty·one

T h e t a t t o o t o o k forever. Alex expected the pain to quit, but each jab startled him and made him draw further into himself. Klema was a good distraction; he brought tapes from the car and told him stories about the crazy characters who lived on his block in Brooklyn, while Phish, then Bela Fleck, played in the background. Finally, Jimbo swabbed away the excess ink one last time and announced, "Coyote's done. Another finished canvas."

Alex stepped into the mirrored cubicle to check out his arm. The silver-blue coyote loped through the chaparral, headed for some secret destination. Alex grinned. "Looks great."

Jimbo peeled off his wrist tape and gloves. "Glad you like it." He winked at Klema. "Change your mind?"

Klema backed away with his hands in front of him. "No way. I'll stick to my earring. It looks good on Alex, though," he added.

Jimbo laughed. "Don't apologize. I understand." He raised a bushy eyebrow at Alex. "I do earrings, too."

"Sure. Next you'll want me to have a navel ring—how about it, Rita?" Alex teased. His sister was standing at the door, braiding her hair.

"Forget it!" she cried. "Dad's going to have enough trouble with this one."

"Don't worry. I'm done—for today, anyway." Alex craned his neck toward the full-length mirror. He couldn't take his eyes off his tattoo, a permanent reminder of the summer that changed his life.

Jimbo bandaged his arm and ran through the usual instructions. "Keep this on for two hours. And remember—no swimming until it heals."

Klema's face fell. "That mean we can't surf?"

Alex swore. "I forgot. You'll have to go with Rita. She can borrow my board—"

Klema's eyes widened as he turned to stare at Rita. "You never told me you could surf."

"You never asked. I'm not as good as Alex—but we can't all be that perfect."

Alex shooed his sister away. "Take the car home," he said, "I'll see you after work."

Klema and Rita left arm in arm. Alex didn't have time to feel left out, because business picked up quickly after that. He was glad, even though working made his arm throb. He didn't want to think about everything he'd done in the last few days. It was too much to absorb all at once.

When it was time for Alex to leave, Jimbo offered him a ride. "I'm having dinner with my daughter tonight," he said. "I go near your place to pick her up."

So Jimbo had a family. Somehow, Alex had never pictured him with a life beyond the tattoo shop—but of course, that was ridiculous.

Jimbo's car was an old Karmann Ghia convertible without a speck of rust, as elegant and funky as some of his tattoo designs. Alex settled back in the passenger's seat, enjoying the feel of the wind whipping through his hair and the rush as they sped down Ocean Avenue, making three lights without a pause. At Ocean and Pico, Jimbo stopped for a red light, resting his decorated arms across the steering wheel. He glanced at Alex. "Things are better today, huh? Nice to have your sister here, and your buddy?"

"Yeah. It's great." The engine idled gently, and Alex was

tempted to tell Jimbo everything. After all, the guy had saved Tito's life and obviously didn't care that Perone was gay. But then the light changed, and the convertible accelerated through the intersection. He'd have to yell, to make himself heard. Besides, knowing Jimbo, he'd probably figured things out already. So Alex settled back in his seat, enjoying the luxury of being driven in a sweet little car through the soft California night, while palm fronds tossed and tangled overhead and low-slung waves coiled up the beach in the distance.

They crossed the line into Venice, and Alex gave Jimbo directions to his house. As they neared his street, his legs began to bounce. He hated the thought of telling his mother. She was so distant and unpredictable. If she got into one of her moods—

Jimbo pulled up behind the Chevy. "Take good care of that tattoo. Your dad will *really* be after my hide now."

Alex laughed. "Hopefully he won't notice. He's kind of a space cadet." He started to climb out, but Jimbo set a hand on his shoulder.

"Alex, that coyote is more than just a nice tattoo design— you have real talent. Have you thought about art school?"

"Not really." Alex suddenly realized that he'd never considered the future at all. Had he planned not to be around? Maybe the present was so complicated, it took up all his time. Things would be different now.

"There are some good programs in the California system. I don't know how long you're planning to stay, but you might want to take a look while you're here," Jimbo said. "Meanwhile, I'm going to feature your coyote in the display box outside, to pull in some younger customers. Okay with you?"

"Great. Thanks a lot." Alex reached over and shook Jimbo's hand. He stood on the curb, watching, until the convertible pulled away. Amazing. An adult who accepted him, no questions asked. Alex drew himself to his full height and walked slowly to the house, gearing himself up for the next round like a boxer in the ring.

§ § §

Music floated from inside: Rita's flute, punctuated with a soft swish swish beat. He went through the kitchen and stood in the living room door, listening. Rita swayed slowly with the jazz riff she was playing, her hair flicking from side to side across her back. Klema kept time with a jar half full of rice, its soft syncopated beat steadying the floating notes of the flute. Klema's eyes were riveted to Rita's face, but hers were closed; she was lost to the music. Chris Beekman sat on the couch, keeping time with his fingers on his bare knees. When he looked at Alex, his smile froze.

"What have you done *now?*" Chris stumbled to his feet and stared at Alex's bandaged arm.

The flute faltered, then stopped, as Rita opened her eyes. She shot Alex a sympathetic look.

"I got a tattoo," Alex said. "Want to see it?"

"Oh, for God's sake." Chris stood up. "Alex, you promised—"

"I know, I know. Changed my mind." Alex peeled off a piece of adhesive and pulled the gauze back. "It's a coyote. I designed it myself."

Chris shielded his eyes with his hand. "Cover that damned thing up! What's it going to be next! Do you have to do something drastic every day!"

Alex cringed, and Rita whispered, "Dad, take it easy—"

Chris Beekman's neck was bright red. "You stay out of this," he snapped at his daughter. Alex and Rita glanced at each other, stunned. Their father never yelled at Rita. Klema set the jar down on the table and looked around anxiously, as if searching for a place to hide. Chris glared at him, then at Rita. "Listen, Rita. Why don't you and your friend take a walk—"

"No," Alex said. "I want them here. I can't do this stuff alone anymore." Saying the words, admitting his need, made him feel suddenly powerful. He smoothed the bandage down and stood poised on the balls of his feet. His father stayed speechless, and finally Alex said, "Look, Dad. I'm sorry about the tattoo, but it's my body. Don't I have the right to decide what to do with it?"

"Maybe when you're eighteen, or living on your own," his father said. "But at long as you live in my house, you follow my rules."

"I see." Alex perched on the armchair. "Do you have rules about my being gay, too?"

To his utter astonishment, his father's chin quivered like a child's. He slumped onto the couch, holding his face in his hands. "I don't know," he said softly.

"Jesus," Alex said. Klema disappeared into the kitchen.

"Dad—" Rita squeezed onto the couch beside her father and put her arm around his neck. "Dad, don't cry."

Chris wiped his glasses on his shirttail. "Sorry. I don't know where that came from." He wiped his eyes and gazed at Alex with a hurt and puzzled expression. "I was up all night, worrying about you. Everything else you've been through, growing up, I could remember myself. Or at least relate to enough so I could help you. But now I'm clueless, as you would say." He tried to smile, but it only made his face seem more twisted.

Rita drew back. "It's no different than with me, Dad. You don't know what it's like to be a girl, either."

"True. I guess—" he gave Alex an awkward pat on the knee. "Maybe I feel you're starting a dangerous journey alone—and I can't come along."

"That may be, Dad. But I'd still like to find you here when I get back." Alex stood up, his heart pounding, and gave his father a quick, awkward hug before taking the phone into his bedroom.

● ● ●

Alex's mother was quiet so long, after he blurted out his news, that he finally asked, "Mom—you there?"

"I am." Her voice was flat, tired. "You know, I'm not surprised. I knew, deep down. I asked Rita about it once, but then I backed away. It frightened me." He heard a scratching sound and realized she was lighting a cigarette. He could imagine her on the other end, waving curls of smoke away from her face with one ringed hand. "It's okay, Alex," she said at last, but he could tell she was forcing herself to be accepting. "Of course I love you, no matter what—"

"I love you, too, Mom." His voice broke.

"Honey," she said. "Don't be upset. It's just—a shock, that's all. Your father and I will have some adjusting to do."

"How about me?" Alex paced the floor. "So far, no one in the family has asked what this is like for *me*. Don't you think that's strange? I mean, *I'm* the one who's gay, Mom."

Dale didn't say anything for a minute. Finally she said, in a voice that was more than three thousand miles away, "I'm sorry, Alex. I guess it's because none of us can quite imagine what it's like. How *does* it feel?"

"Scary," he said. "Exciting. And the biggest relief in my life."

"Relief?"

"Sure, Mom. Think about it. I've been hiding out for seventeen years. Now I can tell you who I really am. Alex, your son. Who's gay."

Dale cleared her throat. "Alex, I need to think about this a little. All kinds of crazy worries are flying around in my head—"

"Like whether I'll get AIDS?"

"Of course. And realizing you might not have children—"

"Mom, Rita could get AIDS, too. Anyone can. And

I've thought about kids. Haven't you seen stories in the paper about gay couples adopting—"

"Whoa, mister. I'm not ready for that concept yet. Or for any of this. Look, why don't we talk again tomorrow. I need to sleep on it."

The conversation was *not* going the way Alex had hoped. He couldn't tell if his mother was angry, sad, or just plain shocked. "Do you want to talk to Dad?" he asked.

"Not tonight." His mother coughed, a deep, throaty sound that told him she'd been smoking too much. "I'm sorry honey. It's a lot to take in, all at once. But I do love you."

"Thanks, Mom. I'll call you tomorrow."

"Hold on." She coughed again; Alex waited until she caught her breath, wishing like hell she could give up cigarettes. "Alex," she said at last, "you're very brave. Lots of people—myself included—have never told anyone the truth about their lives. About who we really are. I admire you for that even if I don't agree with your choice."

She hung up before Alex could explain. He pounded the mattress with his fist. *Don't you see?* he wanted to yell. *It's not a choice. This is who I am!*

He switched on the overhead fan and flopped onto the bed. He had miles to go with this one.

Alex watched the white blades slice the air for a long time, until he recognized his sister's gentle tap on the door: three shorts and two longs. "Come in."

Rita and Klema came in together and sat across from him on the other bed. Rita handed him a bowl of cold pasta with pesto sauce. Alex ate fast, enjoying its sharp, garlicky taste. "How was it?" Rita asked.

"Not so great," Alex said. "She seemed kind of—stunned, I guess. Like I'd given her terrible news." He pushed his hair off his face. "Sometimes I wish I could go backward and start over—but it's too late for that now."

Klema twisted his hands in his lap. "I feel kind of in the way here," he said. "If you want me to stay someplace for a day or two—"

"Forget it!" Rita and Alex said in unison. The three of them burst out laughing.

"You're stuck with us now that you know all the family secrets." Alex finished eating and went to the closet to dig his soccer ball from the mess, determined to return to the sweet, good feelings he'd had when this day began. He tossed the ball to Klema, who caught it against his chest with a grunt. "Come on, it's time for you to start training."

Klema stood up, clutching the ball. "Me? What for?"

"The soccer team, of course," Alex said. "After watching you bike and surf, I realized you're probably good at most sports—especially if you have a black belt. Did you ever play soccer?"

"Not since eighth grade, when I got serious about karate. But come on, Beekman, who wants to join the team just to sit on the bench?"

"You wouldn't," Alex said. "A lot of our best defensive players graduated—including our keeper. You'd make a great goalie. We'll start on the patio tonight, and practice on the beach tomorrow morning." He started for the door, then stopped. Rita was crying. "God, I must look like a werewolf or something. People see me and cry. What's wrong?"

"Nothing." She put her arms around him. "You're just so—" she gulped, then tried again. "You're different. I mean, *good* different. You're the way you were when we were little. For years, I thought I'd lost you. I've been wondering, for so long, where that feisty little kid went."

"He's here." Alex smoothed his bandage tight on his arm. "Come on, Rita," he said, pointing at the ball, "you'll be playing again, too. We'll start with short, quick passes on the concrete."

Rita stopped him in the doorway, her eyes begging. "Does

this mean you're coming home in August?"

Home. There it was again: that loaded word. Alex gave her a sad smile. "Maybe I'm home already." When he saw the hurt in her face, he added quickly, "I don't know yet. It's too soon to tell. Sounds like it's going to take more than a few phone calls to sort things out with Mom, so I'm sure I'll be back later this summer, at least to visit. Don't worry—once I decide, you'll be the first to know."

As they moved the furniture aside on the patio, Alex thought about his choices. If he stayed in L.A., he might be able to hang out with Tito—assuming he could learn to deal with Ken. Right now, he couldn't imagine that.

He could keep learning from Jimbo. Surf with Sly and the Point Zero crowd, who might not call him names, but lived in their own isolated worlds, rarely connecting. He could apply to art schools, maybe find some guys like himself . . .

But there was always the problem of finishing high school. Where? In some new place where he didn't know a soul? Or back in Griswold's "fluorescent prison," as Molly called it? Of course, he could end up cocaptain of the soccer team in Vermont; maybe they'd make state finals this year. He'd have Rita, Molly, and Klema, who wouldn't care if he was gay, or covered with orange stripes—but the rest of the place would tear him apart like sharks. Never mind that now, Alex thought. He'd stay with his father until the middle of August. When it was time for soccer—well, he'd see.

Alex, Rita, and Klema positioned themselves on the edges of the patio. Chris turned on the light and watched from the doorway, sipping a soda while the ball sailed in and out of the shadows, a white spinning sphere like the moon resting overhead. Alex still felt a hollow ache in his chest, the emptiness of losing Tito. But his own raw self was slowly edging into the hole Tito had left behind. With deep concentration, Alex emptied his mind, the way he'd learned to do long ago when running down the line on the soccer field, or when flying, perfectly balanced, at the head of a long, curling tube in the Pacific. The ball went chunk, ker-chunk across the tiny yard. His sister's hair swung from side to side like a gauze curtain billowing in the wind. Klema's stocky legs flashed white as they sliced through the shadows. His father gave him a shy, sweet smile.

Alex smiled back and trapped the ball. As he sent it sailing over to Klema in a careful, looping arc, he suddenly understood what Tito was getting at on the beach that morning. Alex grinned and leaned against the house, letting the sharp stucco wall hold him up while the truth sank in.

Perone was right. He hadn't been searching for Tito at all. He'd been looking for himself: Alex Beekman. Also known as Blue Coyote.

I dream I'm at Point Zero again, paddling out fast through a narrow channel. The waves are clean breaking lefts, just the way I like them. No wind. Out beyond the first line of breakers, I rest alone in a calm patch of water. A chopper hovers above me, wings beating like an angry dragonfly, then sweeps sideways over the mountain.

The waves come at me in sets of two, then three; I'm waiting for the big one. When it arrives, I panic. It's at least a double over-head, a dark green, quivering mass. As it rears up, ready to fling itself at the shore, it becomes a towering, glittering wall as alive and potent as a lover. I force myself to meet it, climb to the crest, and settle into a firm crouch as I slide along the wall just ahead of the break point.

I'm in the barrel. The wave forms a tube whose lip curls over and around me. I skim just ahead of it, knowing if I miss a beat, the wave will bury me, chop me to bits, snap my ankle leash, and grind up my board. I'm riding on the razor's edge between terror and ecstasy, my heart in my throat, too frightened to scream, too excited to shout.

The ocean's power surges up into my body. I start to play with the wave, riding up its curved surface almost to the lip, then turn-ing to take a steep angle down the side of the barrel. My wave seems to be breaking forever along the coast. I think I'm alone in the tube when suddenly, another surfer appears out of nowhere, just ahead. He's perched on a sweet little triple-fin scag, a good head shorter than my six-two Eberly. He scoots up and down the side of the wave like a snowboarder dancing over moguls.

I swoop closer, taking the wave at a steep angle. The guy wears a half wet suit, showing muscular legs and arms, and he's built stocky and square. Is it Tito? No, not with that hair: bleached blond and flyaway, like mine. And that's a beard, isn't it? Hard to tell, with spray and foam flying. Who is he?

He must know I'm here; he plays with me while we cruise the wave, letting me get close, then pulling out fast. He turns and heads up toward the lip; I follow, but I'm too eager to catch him; I overreach and fly over the top in a wipeout. I'm airborne, diving deep to escape my plunging board. The wave breaks beyond me, hitting the beach with a roar that shakes me even underwater.

I come up gasping for breath, reel in my board, and kneel, paddling slowly, looking for the surfer.

He's gone, but I'm not afraid. He'll be back, and so will I. This dream will keep coming, like the wave trains that rise and pound the coast forever; it will come until he's real and I no longer need him in my dreams.